T0366178

DON'T

R.T. SALAS

Order this book online at www.trafford.com
or email orders@trafford.com

Most Trafford titles are also available at major online book retailers.

Printed in the United States of America.

ISBN: 978-1-4907-2253-5 (sc)
ISBN: 978-1-4907-2254-2 (e)

Trafford rev. 12/23/2013

 www.trafford.com

North America & international
toll-free: 1 888 232 4444 (USA & Canada)
fax: 812 355 4082

This is a story of a man who broke a seal not meant to be broken and whose disappearance leaves more questions than answers. The more searching for answers are found the more questions are asked. Before the unfortunate victim's disappearances, behavior was beginning to be more and more elusive. The police search which came out empty handed for suspects only had testimonials from few eyewitness and similar occurrence which happened about a hundred years ago, according to police archives and witness testaments accounts. The same behavior and patters the same disturbances siting's etc. There are all pointing to something else besides common man's doing something more sinister, darker, not meant to be seen by humans. The unfortunate few, who have seen such has got hurt really bad or disappeared without a trace only their cries yelling screaming fading to a dark place unheard of, never be seen or heard from again, never to return. Until a higher group of immortals learn of their broken seal and the disappearances and injuries of people involved. And the untold evil contained escaping only to cause further calamity. They've come to put an end to their terror.

Our story takes place in an old town in the southwest of America, a small town whose name will be unnamed due to privacy issues. The town however is older than the Country it's self. Part of the early frontier settlements if you will. Our unfortunate victim is name is Jim. Jim is an amateur archeologist, he likes to find things and study things, do research and try to find out as much information as he can about his latest find, his latest find was at the cemetery an old looking emblem he found, and this is where our story takes place. It was a late crisp cool fall morning, the leaves are gold and falling and flying all over the place, there is a funeral taking place, an important public official passed away after a long lengthy illness, he is laid to rest. Jim was at the funeral, not attending but there looking to find something of interest, while he is there he'll pay his respect to the recently decease as not to look rude, and then go about his business. As he leaves the mourning people with respect, he looks towards the back of the cemetery. He wondered to the old part of the cemetery where just by looking at the graves, you can tell it's very old and historical. He walked all over till something caught his eye, it was some private mausoleums, one in particular caught his eye, it was made from black marble looked very old and un kept as a matter of fact the whole area needed to be cleaned, but wasn't. As he approached the old building, he saw an old iron rod iron fence around it, as if it was meant to keep something in. the fence was over six feet tall. He looked for the way in and found it, but it was locked, he noticed it had an outdated lock, more than likely the key is long gone. So, he decided to climb the fence, after struggling to get in, he finally did. He then walked around the building carefully and very observantly, looking at the very fine detail, pulling out his camera taking pictures for his archives and personal records. Upon making his way to the front of the building he saw the door, oddly it has no accessible way to get in, no knob, no handle, no nothing to suggest this building was meant to be entered, everything about it suggested that instead of occupants coming in they were to keep from coming out. As Jim was looking, he saw three unique looking emblems in front of the building. One was positioned on the very middle top of the opening of the building the other two are positioned on both sides of the door. The emblems appear to be made from either brass or copper it was hard to tell for him, it is weathered pretty well. So he decided to take photos of the emblems, upon taking photos he noticed there was some inscriptions on them, again due to the weathered condition of the emblems, it is hard to make out what's it reads or what it is. He decided then he is going to remove one of the emblems to clean up and study to learn what kind of inscription, writing, hieroglyphics it might be. So, he started to remove the right side emblem, work on it, as almost as he started to work on loosening the emblem he heard a real gut wrenching scream, coming from above him. It sounded like a big bird, he jumped out of getting startled and stepped back and he looked around, then he looked up, and to his stunning surprise he saw a big vulture black in color looking down at him. This big vulture is unusual around here, he was all black had to have at least an eight foot wide wing span by the look of him. His exposing flesh is dark grey and has these evil glowing red eyes looking at him as if he was peering right through him. And again the big bird let out a really loud scream, this time looking down right at him, as if it was warning him to stay away from the building or not to disturb the emblems, in either case it wanted him out. After looking at it for a while it flew off fairly close to him, he could hear a swoosh of a of air wind go by him almost pushing him to aside. He turned and looked at it fly off and afterwards he continued to work on the emblem, loosening it. After struggling with it he finally worked it free. It was approximately ten inches long, one and a half inches wide, and half inch thick and probably weigh about three to four pounds estimating. He did not realize how much time he spends looking then searching for his latest find to study. He noticed it is getting near dark, he knew it was near mid-morning he was occupied with his find and his encounter. He then got out of the gate, as he was getting out he felt an eerie presents, something he never felt before. He looked around, he saw nothing, but still the feeling was still there. Time was not on his side, as time goes by the quicker it seemed to get darker, so he hurried and got out and headed back to his car. As he was heading back to his car, he heard that awful scream again, he looked up at the trees where he thought he heard the screams and couldn't find anything, and he was specifically looking for that big bird and all he could hear is its cries and the sound of it flying around. As he started to walk faster he bumped into an odd looking lady out of nowhere she had bright red hair and was dressed in old looking clothes, raggedy, suggesting she was either homeless or poor. She looked at him and said "Trouble follows you from here, the kind of trouble that cannot be ignored nor be hidden from, you're doomed." As she was looking at him, he moved around her and walked around and looked at her at a final glanced, then he headed to his car. He got into his car, and left in a hurry, the cemetery with that screaming bird, and odd looking lady gave him the creeps, and on top of that, that other feeling he got that eerie feeling. He just shook it off. As he was leaving the cemetery he looked in the rearview mirror and he saw the reflection of the cemetery and to his shock the big vulture was on a dead tree looking at him leave. As he left he decided he is going to have a cup of coffee so he goes to his favorite diner where he gets off in the cold wind blowing. He enters the dinner where it is much warmer inside and it feels good to be in the company of people, well normal people anyways. As he grabbed a stool at the bar the waitress, Barbra who knew Jim, asked him "What will it be Jim?" smiling Jim said "Barbra, I'll have a large coffee black." As he looked around for a short while, looking at all the people carrying on their conversations, the waitress handed him his coffee. "Here you go Jim." taking his coffee, he turned to Barbra and said "Thanks." As he started to drink his coffee he was looking at his car parked outside. The wind was still blowing and the sky was beginning to get overcast as the snow is approaching. During that time while he is having his coffee, at the cemetery, at the mausoleum where he was at, where he removed the emblem, the door opens up a little from the inside. The sky is still visible because of the city's skylights and the overcast of clouds. As a result the mausoleum has a very pale light coming from the city lights something that is not supposed to come out is coming out that has not come out for a very long time. This thing almost looks the grim reaper, but has no sickle. Making its way out of the gate, it broke through the lock holding the gate closed in search of the one who took the emblem. The emblem is a seal that is meant to keep them at bay, keep them in the mausoleum. Oddly as the deathly figure moved about he made no noise when it moved about. As it made it ways to the front of the cemetery, it looked at the vulture that was waiting for it, the vulture looked at it back then it took off towards the center of town in search of the one who broke and took the seal. Meanwhile back at the café Jim was enjoying his coffee, when he finished his cup turned around and said to Barbra "Let me have another one, please" Barbra the waiter walked up saying "Coming up." She poured more coffee in his cup and Jim then started to take another sip of coffee until he noticed that big black bird he saw at the cemetery on top of his car looking in the cafe window looking at him. To his disbelief the big bird was screaming even louder and this time it was scratching with it claws the top of his car scratching the paint off revealing the metal underneath. He could tell it was not happy and wanted to physically harm him. He turned to a guy next to him asking him" Hey did you see that?" pointing at the window towards his car. The guy next to him turned to him looked at him, then looked where he was pointing then looked at that direction and just saw his car. Then he asks "The car?" Jim looked again and saw the big bird was gone, and then he said "No, there was something on top of the car, a big bird scratching it." The guy looked at him and said "No, I do not see any big bird." Jim sat there kind of scared, and puzzled. "Maybe it's just my imagination working overtime, anyways I'm tired." He quietly said to himself. He took another sip of coffee and then he noticed again that same big black bird on top of his car scratching and this time pecking. The pecking the bird is doing is harder than the scratches themselves, and more damaging, the pecks are so hard the look as if a center punch was used. Much to his shock he quickly tugged on the guy next to him and said "Look" At that the guy looked and again saw nothing. "Are you sure you're ok?" He asked. "I don't know." Jim replied. Looking outside the window he was hesitant to go outside, but determined to show he was not just imaging things. He got up went outside did not see the big bird and so he went to his car and much to his suspected fear there he saw the marks, the big bird left behind. The deep scratches and deep center punch like pecks on top of his car, this is minor damage to his car. But this is proof. He went inside the café and told the guy "I'll show you, the damage that thing just caused to my car." He went outside with the guy next to him following and a few more curious spectators. They all went outside and then Jim pointed, at the top of his car, and he asked "Now do you believe me?" The guy looked at the damage and then looked at Jim, and asked him "All this was just caused in such a short while?" Nodding his head Jim said "Yes" The guy then shook his head, and said "Something's mad at you." At that moment everyone who was looking at the car heard the same awful scream as Jim did when he was at the cemetery. One of the onlookers said "Damn! We best go inside, don't know what that is, but it don't sound friendly." Then they all went inside. Jim was in the café for just a while longer pondering on just what happened, he finally developed the nerve to go outside, get in his car and go home. On his way home he had thoughts going through his head, of all the events that went through today, on his way home, he had that eerie feeling again of that presents around the area, and was worse it just happen to be in his neighborhood. As he got out of his car he heard that scream again he looked around did not see any bird but could still hear it and hear it disturb all other birds in the neighborhood, they all are flying away, and he could hear the big swoosh its wings are making as it flaps its wings all over the neighborhood. Nervously he rushed in to his house then he locked the door. Taking a deep breath he thought if it wasn't quite a good idea to remove something like that. Then he reasoned with himself, wait I'm a part time archeologist, I'm not superstitious. I gather nothing but facts, not folk lore, fairy tales, etc. My hobby is based on fact not beliefs. Jim decided to settle for the night, he was tired from all the excitement today and all the physical climbing and physical moving he did today, so in the morning I'm going to have the photos developed and see just what these objects really mean. So he got the film and inserted it into its package and have it ready for tomorrow to take to the photo lab and onto the public library to find out about the inscriptions. In the meantime, he's cleaned up the emblem removing the tarnish it had built up over time, and just finds out what kind of metal these are made of. Upon cleaning the emblem his first initial thought of the type of alloy was incorrect, it is in fact made from bronze. The emblem is now very clean and polished, the inscriptions are now clear, readable, and nevertheless he could not read nor decipher them. He took photos of the now clean emblem for record keeping. It was late into the night and now he is sleep so he went to bed. During his sleep some time in odd parts of the morning he was woken only to hearing scratching on the side of his house, the same kind of scratches he heard before. This is beginning bother him, so he grabbed something to throw at that big bird to go away, hoping it will go away Instead of responding in retaliation. He put on his robe and slippers and went outside on the side of the house, to confront this big bird, when he went to where the scratches were heard, to his relief it was just the branches of his tree he never had a chance to trim that is rubbing on the side of his house. So with much relief again he went back inside his house, closed the door and locked it. As he shut the door behind him, not far away was the vulture looking at him going in, he was on to top one of the trees across the street looking, when the door closed it flew off towards the cemetery. After the little false alarm Jim went to bed fell asleep, with no disturbance throughout the rest of his sleep. Meanwhile Jim is sleeping the vulture is flying to the cemetery and flies to the hooded death figure where they stay facing one another for a while, while they are facing each other. The vultures red eyes peering in the dark faceless hood front of the death figure, they are telepathically communicating about the one who broke and took the seal, and his whereabouts and finally his place of address. The death figure then turns and goes back to the mausoleum and goes inside, the door however remains open. The vulture remains outside the mausoleum on top of the roof. Morning breaks and Jim gets up, has breakfast and sets out to do what he has planned to do for the day. As steps outside he sees a cloudy sky, the weather is getting worse its bringing in the snow, winter is about to set in, the calm wind is cold and almost every leaves from the trees has just about fallen off. As he heads into town, he starts to back up from his drive way, looking through the rearview mirror, to his shock he sees the hooded death figure at the end of the drive way. He slams the brakes opens the door and gets out and looks towards the end of the drive way, to his surprise he sees nothing, but he is quite certain on what he saw. This figure is all black with no face standing around eight feet tall, it didn't have the sickle. But it was standing right in the middle of his driveway. He looked around to see if it moved elsewhere or someone is playing a joke, but it was no joke, and it was nowhere to be found. Nervously Jim got back in his car backed up and went to town, to him this second thing to appear is even more frightening than the first, but who is going to believe him? As he drove off from his home he had to look once more through his rearview mirror and to his shock again he saw that death figure behind him from a distant leaving him behind, this to freaky he thought to himself. As drove off he didn't even want to look in the mirror, he just drove until he stopped at the photo shop, delivered his film. Jim asked the sales man "How long till it's done?" the sales man said "Oh, about an hour." Jim then nodded as he walked out he said "I'll be back by lunch time." And then he waked off, "Ok" the sales man said before the door closed. As Jim was going towards his car, he looked at last night's damage that was done on the top of his car. He still can't believe this had happen so he drove off to the library to find information on the inscription he had found. As he entered the library he bumped into that odd lady once more, and she looked at him, looked at him as if something was about to happen to him she struggled to speak finally she spoke "You!, your doomed to go into the recesses of darkness never to return." Looking at her he moved out of the way and as he did he told her "Lady shut the hell up." And he walked off into the archives section of the library. Walking off but still turning back to the lady, he couldn't help but to ponder those words she spoke of. Jim turned forwards the direction he is walking, soon he made his way to the part of the library where the city's archives are. So, on with his search, looking for clues and origins of the emblems he has. During his search he discovered more interesting facts, the more he looked up the past, the deeper and sinister it seemed to get. He found an old book containing early foreign settlers, and their recorded origins and heritage, there was an emblem that looked like the one he has, but a little different, it didn't have much, only the settlers did not socialize much with the locals, they kept to themselves, there was few of them, he saw early photos, the photos are very old and difficult to make out the features of the family with the similar looking emblem. Nevertheless one can see it is two brothers and one sister a family dog and a big bird. As he looked deeper, into this specific family, more and more things start coming to light, countless and countless accusations of witchcraft sorcery and every imaginable practice of the black arts, but none could be proven so they were acquitted on several occasions. The origins of this family were unknown, only that they come from the old world Europe, but there are lots and lots places in Europe, so there is where the search goes cold. Did they come to the new world as escapees? Or exiles, or simply looking for a better life, or star a new one, no one knows. As he was looking, and reading book after book, he noticed the lights were unusually dim, like of after hours, he looked around and saw no one, as if the place is closed for the day he looked around to see if he could find any one, but no one, was around. Much to his confusion, he was walking around and went back to the archival books in the library to retrieve his belongings and leave, and there is where he saw his horrific encounter. In front of him no less than ten feet standing in front on him towering over him, standing around eight feet tall, all black featureless, hooded, faceless, dark entity, stood, the same deathly figure he saw in his rear view mirror. He froze out fear, he could not believe his eyes, as he tried to move sideways, and the death figure counteracted him. He moves as if he didn't want him to go anywhere, after some moving side and back and corner running, everywhere he tried to go, turning right in front of him was the death figure cutting him off. As he tried several routs he was eventually cornered. Trapped and unable to yell for help he stood there petrified as the deathly entity closed in. them he stopped, looking down at him, "Wh, wh, what do you want?" asked Jim. As he was looking into the dark empty hood, he could barely hear an unearthly low moan saying "Return or be doomed." At that, all of a sudden, everything went back to normal, the lights are on people are everywhere, and the deathly entity is gone. To his relieve, he thought he was having a bad dream that seemed so real. As an educated man, he doesn't believe in folklore or ghost or anything supernatural, so he dismissed it as a bad dream. He looked at his watch and a couple of hours passed by and it is near lunch time, so he goes back to the photo lab and gets his pictures and he calls his friend Jeff. Jeff is a friend of Jim, they met in a collage and became friends ever since, Jim is an accountant in a firm and Jeff is a C.E.O. of a local bank. They met for lunch at a restaurant, as they put in their order, Jim said to Jeff, "Hey, I have something to show you, take a look." Jim pulls out the photos and shows Jeff, Jeff then looks at them. One by one, slowly looking at them, until the last one, then he put them down and he had a curious look on his face, them he asked "What is this?" Jim said "This is my latest find, I'm still looking into the origins of it, I kind of know where it might of come from and might of have it, but the writings or inscriptions, not yet." Looking at the photos again, he asked "Where did you find them?" Jim said with a smile "Well let's just say, it was off an old building." "Historic?" asked Jeff. "Kind of." Jim said. The waiter brought their meals, and then they ate their lunch. After lunch as they left the restaurant Jeff said to Jim "Let me know how your latest find goes, it looks interesting, historic." Then Jim said "Sure, yes I will." Then each left their own separate ways, Jeff went back to his bank, and Jim went back doing more research. Jim decided to walk to the library, instead of driving, the library was not far from the restaurant they just ate in. As Jim walked the sidewalks looking at the windows to the apartment stores and the displays they had in them, he saw something in the reflection of one of the windows, what he saw was other than his reflection he saw again the deathly figure behind him, and it looks as if he was behind a car that's parked on the side of the side walk, he turned around to see and saw nothing. Slowly but surely he started back towards the library to look up what inscriptions on the emblems. He was looking continuously and found nothing, and then he used the library's computers to find all known writings, hieroglyphics, etc. So far his search has come out empty handed. The day was getting late and the library was soon to close for the day, so Jim started to head home. As he stepped out of the library, he felt a really chilly gust of wind, unusually cold, and yes the weather is cold but this is a different cold, a supernatural cold. As he continued walking he heard in the somewhat gust of wind that unearthly low moan say "Return or be doomed." He looked around and to his surprise he saw the deathly figure again from a distant looking at him. He was close to his car, he quickly got in and drove off, as he dove off again in his rearview mirror he can see the deathly figure standing in the middle of the street looking at him drive off. What's so strange are the people in the background walking around as if they didn't see the deathly figure nor felt the cold gusts of wind, they were in fact walking on like in everyday life. Some were walking in front and behind it. He speeds towards his home and quickly got off and ran inside his house and locked the door. And sat on his couch thinking of what he just saw and all what has happened to him in last few hours. As he sat there he pondered it must be his imagination, because he can see it, the deathly figure and no one else can. He pulled out the photos and looked then once more and was scrutinizing them. He saw looking at them in silence, it was so quiet, and was intense until he jumped when his phone started to rig. It is his friend Jeff who is calling. "Hello," Jim said. "Jim did you uh ever found out, what the inscriptions mean or deciphered them?" Jeff asked, over the phone. "No, not yet, I'm still looking." Jim said. "Well, I have an acquaintance of mine that can probably help." Jeff said. Exiting Jim said "Great, that's good news, thanks." Then Jeff said "Hey, um I need to borrow some of those photos you took of your find." "Ok" said Jim. Then Jim asked "Who is your acquaintance." Then Jeff said "He is a professor who I met in a seminar, and he happens to know about languages and writings." "Oh ok, awesome, thanks" said Jim. Then Jeff said "Ok, I'll be by sometime tomorrow, is that fine?" "Sure." Jim said. As Jim hung up the phone he again looked at the photos, them he thought to himself his friend apparently is also interested in his find also. As night fell in and Jim was getting ready to go to bed he had the emblem once more in his hands holding it looking at it, looking at the inscriptions. Thinking of its significant, its original purpose, its design, and finally its maker, and designer. He put the emblem away, and then he went off to bed. As he was trying to sleep he was looking out the window, and could see the moonlight coming through the cast clouds above, then darkness all of a sudden came over the entire window, he had a good idea what it might be, the deathly figure outside looking in, he got up from his bed and went to other windows to confirm his suspicion and much to his surprise it was in fact the clouds had covered the moon completely. He sighed of relief. So back to bed he went and fell fast asleep without further interruptions. Meanwhile he was in his cozy bed, the deathly figure went back to the cemetery towards the back where the mausoleum is. There, the vulture stood upon the roof top of the mausoleum, looking down at him. It went inside the mausoleum, only for another equally horrific figure to come out. This other figure just as tall the first he has the appearance of a tall heavy walking skeleton face pale bone with a black worn out trench coat and a long black hat, with gloves, it has the appearance of been dead long since dead flesh rotted off to exposing bone. When it walks, its steps can be felt and heard, a heavy stomper stepper. As he stomped out stepping out, it turned and looked at the vulture. The vulture with the evil red glowing eyes, looking in to his eye sockets that seem to have no eyes in place of them, only empty cavities where they once were, nevertheless it could still see and hear, and probably not speak. Judging by its sheer size it looks like it has a lot of strength even though it's been dead for quite some time now. As it looked at the vulture, it turned towards town and started walking and its stepping so heavy or powerful or perhaps both, could be heard as it heads off towards town. All through the night the clouds covered the moon, and then it started to snow, the fact that it is cold and snowing makes no never mind to the tall walking skeleton, already making its way to Jim's house. All the way to his place his stepping being heavy and powerful that it is, could be felt and heard. Morning arrived and Jim was woken up by what he thought were small shakes from a distant getting closer, then it stopped. He got out of bed looked out the window, and all he could see is the neighborhood covered in snow with it still snowing, and a couple of dogs barking loud, but then again, dogs in this neighborhood bark loud at just about anything, including stray alley cats, so he quickly dismisses it. As he was washing up and getting ready for today's activities, his friend Jeff called and told him to meet him at the restaurant where they last ate, which was yesterday. As Jim was getting ready to leave he heard the next door neighbor's dog bark with a sense of panic because it was going in and out of its dog house. Jim paid no never mind to it, he just got in his car and backed out his driveway and drove off. As he was driving off he couldn't help but think of that deathly figure he saw yesterday, so out of anticipation he looked through his rear view mirror and much to his shock he saw that tall skeleton standing near his house with the neighbor's dog holding it by the chain up almost to its shoulder height, while the dog was struggling to break free and struggling to breath. Jim could not believe what he just saw, he slammed the brakes of his car, rolled the window down and looked back, by that time the dog was running with the chain dangling behind it. He got back in and drove off rolling up the window thinking he must be seeing things. He drove to the restaurant to meet his friend and his acquaintance. As drove up he stopped, parked and stood still, and was hearing very closely and he could hear was nothing, too quiet of a nothing. Perhaps the snow acted like a sound insulation and quieted all incoming sounds he was especially trying to hear those heavy stomping footsteps he heard at his house. After observing the quietness he walked in, and looked around and he saw his friend waiving at him flagging him down. He headed towards the table and up his arrival both his friend and his acquaintance stood up and greeted him. Jeff said "Jim, I want you to meet Professor Sunnor." Both shook hands Jim said" Please to meet you sir, I'm Jim." Shaking Jims hand he said "David." Then they all sit down, they ordered breakfast and coffee, after receiving coffee David said to Jim, "Jeff here tells me you have a find, an interesting piece with some kind of writings inscriptions." Then Jim said "Oh, yes, here take a look, at these photos, I took of this finding." At that David put on his half glasses and looked at the photos one by one, when he finally finished looking at the photos he said "Wow, this really is very interesting, the writing though it looks something like a hunters/keepers writings, not exactly the same as but something like it." David stayed looking at it, and then he asked him, "Where did you acquire this piece, if you don't mind me asking?" Jim said "I found it on a very old building." Then David said "Ah, ok a historic item then," Then David pulls out an old book which contained different writings and inscriptions and their meanings. As he looked through he compared and after a while he closed his book and said," This might be different, it looks different it looked something like this one," David opened his book and showed the pictures of the writings the time periods, the meanings, the, purpose, the history. David then said, "It looks similar to this, these are from Europe and they are hunters of injustices and sought out to right a wrong, however this is different, it looks European and its different, time period almost the same predating American settlements." David turns to Jeff and said "This is unique to find this in an American town on an old building its pretty unique, it has to have a great significant to it." Then David asked Jim, "Do you mind letting have a photo of this?" "Sure." Jim said. So Jim gives him a copy of one of the photos. Then David said 'I know a historian who knows all about this, he studies ancient languages, artifacts, and stuff like this." He put the photo in his coat pocket and they ate their breakfast. After a lengthy conversation they departed and before David was to leave he turned to Jim and said "I'll be in touch, give me a few days, and I'll have a defendant answer, I'm very curious to know also." At that they all shook hands and departed. As Jim got in his car, he whistled to his friend Jeff, then Jeff came over and asked "What's up Jim?" then Jim said "Hey I think I've been seeing real creepy things, unusual creepy things." With a puzzled look on his face Jeff asked Jim" Like what?" sighing Jim said "This morning I thought I saw a tall walking body with a tall hat with a skull face near my house looking at me." "What? You're joking, right?" said Jeff. Shaking his head Jim said "No, there's more." Looking at his friend with uncertainty, he asked "What?" Then Jim said "A couple of days ago, I saw the grim reaper without his sickle blade, but before that I saw a big black bird that looks like a vulture with glowing red eyes." Not knowing rather to believe his friend or not he asked "Are you under a lot of stress?" "No" Jim said. Then Jeff stood back then said "This is not kike you to say things like this." Looking back at his friend Jim said "I know I know, but I'm telling you what I saw." Then Jeff said "Try to relax, you sound tense, I have to go, but I'll call you later on, ok? Nodding his head Jim said "Fine." Then he drove off, it started to snow a little heavier so he decided to not go back to his house, because what he saw this morning he was still disturbed, so decided he was going driving around town and he happens to drive pass by the cemetery as he did he slowed down, something caught his eye, the same tall walking skeleton was at the cemetery walking the graves as he pass by slowly the skeleton turned his head towards him still walking, and he could hear his heavy powerful footsteps. As he stopped his car the skeleton also stopped walking and turned fully faced towards him in his car. He could only see partial part of his upper body the other was behind the tombstones. They both stared looking at each other. There in the middle of a mild snow fall they stood a distant apart looking at each other. Jim was frozen out of fear, he has never not even in his wildest imagination could ever picture such a site, he got some courage to step out of his car, took a few step forward and stop and yell at it "What do you want from me?, why do you keep bothering me?" Then there was silence for a few seconds then to Jims horror the skeleton figure pulled out a chain, he could hear the chain gangling as he pulled it up, and the neighbor's dog was at the end of it, already dead, the dog was in fact a large dog, cannot easily picked up by a person, but this is not an ordinary person here, it is what it seems it used to be a person. The skeleton figure with one swing throws the dog's dead carcass towards Jim hard throwing him hard against his car hard making a light dent on the cars door side. The impact knocks Jim off his feet and knocks the air out of Jim. Barely getting up Jim pushed the dog's dead body off of him he struggles to breathe in panic, has enough strength to get up and get in his car and drive off peeling out. As he drives off he's even more scared and now getting paranoid, he drives fast he passes by the police station, slams his brakes and goes back and decides to stop and tell the police exactly what happened to him. As he got off he could barely hear the heavy footsteps again coming his way. He quickly dashed to the doorway to the police station, as he entered he approached the front desk where an officer who was doing paperwork. "Yes sir what can we do for you today?" Still shaken up, he struggled to speak, with the officer looking, slowly nodding." "Yes" Said the officer. "I, I, would like to speak with someone." Jim said finally. Still looking at him, the officer asked him "What exactly about?" then Jim said "Something not normal." Looking at him with his head tilted aside as if he knew nothing he told him "Ok, just have a seat over there and someone will be with you shortly," Nodding Jim sat down on the chairs in front of the front desk. He waited almost thirty minutes and was falling asleep then he heard the front desk officer call him "Hey buddy, hey buddy, a detective will see you now." At that Jim got up and looked the front desk officer pointed to their hallway and said "Right this way, through this door." When he got up he waked up he met the detective "Hello, my name is Detective James Smith" they both shook hands. The detective is a man of recognition, and stature, he is a former military officer retired who was special ops, or Special Forces, who's done special missions etc., something important to with the government, he is a man who stands about six foot four, and is strong and well-disciplined in all his duties now working as a detective. They went to his office. They both sat down and then the detective said "Now, tell me what happened." Jim said "I got assaulted." The detective said "Assaulted?" Jim said "Yes and possibly stalked also." "When you say stalked you mean by the same person who assaulted you?" The detective asked. Jim nodded. "Ok, how did this person look like?" asked the detective. "Um, I don't know, it's hard to describe, how he looked like." Jim said. "You got assaulted and you don't know how your assaulter looks like? The detective asked. The detective then had a puzzling look on his face and then he asked him "Are you pulling my leg son? Because if you are, I'm not amused." Jim said "No, no I'm not pulling your leg detective look." Jim then pulled up his shirt and showed the detective the now forming bruise imprinted **over his chest and said. "I am having trouble breathing." After looking at it, the detective said "Ok,** now, let's start by his appearance, how he looks like." Jim stood looking at him then the detective said "Ok, Fundamental questions, first how tall is he?" Jim said "Over eight feet," the detective looked into his eyes and said "Over eight feet?" Jim nodded. Then the detective asked "Ok, is his built: slender, heavy, and regular?" Jim then said "It's hard to tell, it was snowing. "Looking at Jim he said "Hmm? What race is he, Caucasian, Latino, Black, Asian, other?" then Jim said "He had a skeleton face on." "Skeleton face on?" the detective asked. Jim then nodded. "So, then he was wearing a mask?" the detective said "I believe so." said Jim, but Jim knew it was not a mask, nor a gimmick it was real and very menacing and out to get him. Then the detective said "I don't have much to go on son, only a tall man or person in a supposedly Halloween mask, and or costume, who assaulted you leaving you a big bruise in your entire upper torso." Jim then nodded "I know, but that's what happened." "How did he assault you?" asked the detective. Then Jim said "He threw my neighbor's dog at me, hard," "He threw your neighbor's dog at you?" The detective asked. Jim nodded. "How big is this dog?" asked the detective. Jim said "A large dog weighing at least one hundred fifty pounds at least." "Lift up your shirt again." The detective told Jim. Jim lifted up his shirt by then the bruises darken in color to dark purple and blue. "Did this happen in your neighborhood or house?" asked the detective. "No it happened at the cemetery." Jim answered. Looking at him oddly the detective repeated "The cemetery." At that the detective got his coat and said "Come with me, were going to the emergency, your bruise is getting worse, and I wonder if your ribs are broken or cracked, because you're having trouble breathing." As they went outside, Jim was heading to his car then the detective said "No, no, were going on the squad car were coming back." Jim asked the detective to come look at the damage done to his car by a big bird, and the dent he made by the impact of the dog thrown at him hesitantly, the detective went to look. To his astonishment he looked at Jim and said, "No bird can do this, this looks as if someone took a counterpunch tool and some kind of blade to make these deep scratches and dents, and as far as this dent goes, a real good hit can make this." As the detective waked back to the squad can he said "Come on lets go." So Jim walked back to the detective and got in back of the police car with a police officer driving and the detective on the front passenger seat. Soon they arrived at the hospital, in the emergency the doctor on shift took some x rays of his entire chest area, and now returning with the results. "Ok, these are our patients x-rays, of his chest and no bone cracking, just highly stressed to the brink but a lot of trauma in the flesh tissue." The detective asked the doctor" What can cause this kind of injury?" then the doctor said "Well, it's very blunt, too massive to pinpoint a single part to single damage, but it had to hit him pretty hard, there's bruising in his lungs also." Then the detective asked "Can let's say throwing a large dog at him do that?" the doctor then looked at him and said "If you're talking about an animal running into a man at a high rate of speed, yes, it can, but the angle here, suggests he hit him sideways, like rib to rib." Then the detective said "Well what I'm saying is, if a person threw a dog sideways to another person hard it can cause this." The doctor said "Yes, but one would have to be exceptionally strong, to lift a dog, a large one at that and throw him, were talking about dead weight, he's very fortunate it didn't hit him another angle." "Ok, thanks doctor." The detective said. Both the detective and Jim went back to the station, by then nightfall has already begun to fall in, they went back into his office, and then the detective said "I have a couple of more questions for you." So they both sat down the detective at his desk and the Jim in front of him. "Are you in some kind of trouble?" The detective asked. "No." Jim said shaking his head. Then the detective asked "Do you owe anybody a debt?" Again Jim shaking his head said "No." "Ok, then I think were done for right now, but I'll keep in touch, here my card, if you see your attacker again call me." "Thank you Detective Smith." Jim said. "You bet." The detective said. Then Jim left the police station and soon back to his home, he stopped by a fast food restaurant and took a carry out. He went back to his house, and went inside locked the door, and settled in for the night. As he was eating the phone rang, it was his friend Jeff. "Hello." Jim said. "Hey Jim, how are you, I called you earlier today, but no answer." Jeff said. "Well I had to go to the hospital, then the police station." Jim said. "What happened?" asked Jeff. "You will not believe me if I told you." Jim said "Tell me anyways." Jeff said. Then Jim started to speak" Another thing is after me, it's a big heavy walking skeleton with a trench coat and a long black hat." "Hmmm." Said Jeff "And it threw the neighbor's big dog at me almost breaking my ribs and busting my lungs." Jim said. "I don't know what to tell you, Jim" Said Jeff. Then Jim said "I told you wouldn't believe me." Jeff said "Ok, you need to rest it's quite obvious you have one hectic day." "Alright, I'll speak to you tomorrow." Jim said. "Alright then tomorrow." Jeff said. After he hung up the phone he settles for the night, goes to bed to rest, but his rest is short lived. Soon he hears those dreaded heavy footsteps again from a far coming ever so close. He knows what it is, that's coming his way, and the fear in him is building up. He still in pain from earlier during the day when that tall heavy walking skeleton threw the neighbor's dog at him. Now he can't imagine just what that thing is going to do to him this time. His heart starts to pound hard as he can hear and feel the ever so getting close loud stepping and heavy stomping coming close. Finally it's in his yard outside the house, and what's odd is, there is no neighbor's dog barking. As the stomping approach outside the house, it stopped. He waited in fear, waited in silence, and just as quick as it stopped it starts. The stomping continues he could now feel and hear it going outside around the house. As he hears the stomps he's looking through the window, and as soon as he hears the stomps coming close to the window it blocked the window, the big heavy walking skeleton has blocked the partially cast covered moon is now blocked from his window. And the stomping stops. And dead silence for at least a minute. Then it continues to around the house, while it's going around the house, it starts to hit against the house. The hits are so loud, they sound as if they're going to break through the walls, then the hitting against the walls stop, and then the stomping sounds fade away. As the stomping's continues the fading of the heavy steps are also fading with it. At the sign that the stomping is no longer there, he still feels fear and tense, after a while of silence and nothing happening he finally feels drowsy, and he finally falls asleep. He sleeps sitting down on the chair in his room, with the table. While he sleeps, uneasy, but sleeping the big walking skeleton makes its way back to the cemetery, along the way making those heavy stomping steps, that seem to attract some people still awake during those hours of the night. It arrives back to the cemetery, and goes back to the mausoleum. The door to the mausoleum still opened, as it approached the doorway, it stopped turned around looked towards the city for a moment then peered in the dark doorway, and out comes another horrific figure. This figure is not as big as the previous two, but just as menacing nonetheless. It is in fact a female, a lady whose appearance looks as she's been long sense dead. She is dressed in black clothing, a dress that is moth eating and, almost falling apart. Her style of clothes is that of the early eighteenth century. Her face her flesh looks dried and decayed almost ready to fall off, but her facial features are still intact. She is a tall as a man about six feet even and with long black unkempt hair. Her eyes pitch black, as if she's peering right through a soul. As she steps out, she looks around then she looks up to the tall skeleton, which is looking once more towards the town. Then it turns looks down to her and looks at her with no eyes right into her own eyes. Then both turn up to the vulture on top of the mausoleum with his glowing red eyes, while looking, the big bird makes menacing sounds while they look into its own eyes, then the dead lady sets off the direction of town. The lady, she is much quicker, and faster, quieter than the one before her, she is capable of speaking and making a very wicked crying and laughs. She walks off with walking speed, and starts to make unusual whimpering sounds. The skeleton watches her leave, and then it goes inside the mausoleum. Meanwhile at Jim's house, though out the night with no interruptions. Morning breaks, and it's a new day, he has over slept. After a restless night prior to that he had an eventful day. He woke up in the same position he fell asleep in. Still alarmed, and alert, and still shaken he gets up and washes up and gets ready for the day. Jim feels sluggish this morning, he seems not to get things together, and it might be due to the fact of the events that has been taking place the past few days. Without realizing, paranoia was starting to settle in with Jim. He is starting to lose his logical sense of thinking and his nerve, now even the slight shadows are starting to bother him. Meanwhile at the cemetery, a pedestrian whose name is Jason walking and reading the tombstones, he was reading the names birth dates death dates and possible causes of deaths. Upon reading the stones he wondered to the back of the cemetery, where the mausoleums are, looking at them one by one, looking at the family names and possible family crests, as he was reading, he walked up upon the one where Jim had taken the emblem from. He saw the door and the emblems around it, with one missing, the door was open half way, due to the weathers and the cast skies he had trouble seeing inside the door from outside the tall fence around it. As he stayed looking trying to peer though, the darkness inside he heard an unearthly moan which made his hairs on his back stand up, it was coming from the inside the mausoleum. Then without warning and very quick speed a figure came out with a lot of force, all he could see was a blurry big skull coming at him, the force bent the fence hitting him knocking him several feet back. As he landed, he hit a tombstone knocking unconscious. Then it went back inside the mausoleum with a growl and closed the door from the inside. It might have been sometime before someone noticed him in the cemetery, help was called and he was taken to the hospital. As he slowly started to regain conscience, he looked around and the doctor who saw Jim was at his side. "Hey there, how are you feeling?" asked the doctor. Looking around Jason said "I'm hurting real bad, from all over." Then the doctor walked up to the x ray holder and put up x ray pictures of his body, turned on the back lights and looked and said "Young man, you have a few cracked bones from your legs to your ribs to your upper arms." Then the doctor tuned to him and asked him "Did you hit something or something hit you?" then Jason said "I was thrown back, I know you do not believe me, but it's true." The doctor looked at him with a strange look, because he remembered Jim's injury, which was also that of a high impact hit. The doctor then asked him "Do you know who hit you?" "Well kind of." Jason said. Then the doctor asked him "Would you like to speak to a detective about this?" having trouble moving, Jason stood still then he thought, then he said "Yes I would please." So the doctor nodded and left his room went to his office and called Detective James Smith. Jason dosed off because of the meds he was given, then after a little while he was woken up by the sound of two men having a conversation, walking up closer to his room. They sounded a little garbled to him, because he was still had some the meds in his system. The doctor and the detective arrived and walked into his room. The doctor said to Jason "Jason, I want you to meet Detective James Smith, he'll be talking care of the matter for you." Jason then nodded without saying anything. The detective pulled a curtain around the bed where Jason is lying down. Then he pulls up a chair and then he proceeds to ask questions. "I understand you were thrown a pretty lengthy distant. "The detective said to Jason. Barely being able to speak, Jason said "yes." Then the detective asked "Do you know your attacker?" looking at Jason's face, the detective can see there is something obviously wrong. Having trouble speaking, the detective could barely hear but understand what Jason said "He had a skeleton face." Looking at him the description he gave him was similar to that of Jim's. Just to make sure the detective asked a couple of more questions "how tall is he?" Jason looked at the detective and stared at the window for a while, and then the detective said "Hello? How tall is he, do you know?" Jason turned to the detective and said "Tall and very fast, and strong, to do this to me." And then he started to breath heavy. The detective said "Ok, calm down, calm down, just one more question." Then looking at Jason concern he asked "Where did this happen?" With a much weakened voice Jason said "In the cemetery, the old part." Then Jason closed his eyes and fell back to sleep. The detective stood up, put the chair away leaned over and said

DON'T

with a softer voice "Just relax there, ok, no one in going to do nothing to you anymore." Then he walked out, he them got on his cell phone called the station and had an officer stationed, outside the room where Jason is in. Meanwhile at Jim's house its midmorning and Jim has not moved from his room, what he just went through really played a number on him, there he was sitting down in utter silence, just sitting there like a lifeless zombie hardly moving. The vision of the vulture, the death without a sickle, the tall heavy walking skeleton that killed the neighbor's dog, and threw it at him very hard and fast, all these events kept playing in his head over and over again. Jim is sitting there alone in utter silence then the silence is shattered by a loud knock. Him jumped from his zombie state, confused shaken up, started to get scared again. He heard the knocking once more, he got the nerve to answer the door, he looked through his peep hole in the door, much to his relief it was Detective James Smith. Jim opens the door, slowly with a chain still latched on, looking at the detective, the detective looked at him and asked "Jim, can I come in?" Jim nodded and opened the door, and the detective walks in. The detective said "Excuse me for saying this, but it's kind of dark in here, can you let in some light? It seems a little depressing." At that Jim opened the shutters and curtains. "Thank you." Said the detective they both sat down in the dining table and the detective looked at him with a concern look. That concern look made Jim more nervous, and he started to feel a sense of panic, then the detective said "Jim, I have some not so good news to share with you." At that Jim sunk into his chair and a deep dark feeling went over him. Then he looked up at the detective and asked "You don't believe me, do you?" Still with a concern look on his face the detective said "Had that been the case I wouldn't of come here, I would of send a squad car to pick you up, no I do, because there is another victim you're skeleton attacked, and he got it worse than you did." Jim looked as if he didn't know what to say. He finally said "Attacked? How? Like me." Then the detective said "Apparently there is one who has anger issues or just likes to throw things around including dogs and people," looking at Jim, the detective asked "Have you been out today?" Jim just shook his head. "Ok" said the detective. The detective got up and said "I'm going to your neighbor's house to ask them about their dog." At that he got up and walked out, as he

21

walked out the front door, he turned around and said "Just stay in touch, ok?" Then he walked off to his neighbor's house and knocked at their door. Jim turned to the front of his yard it was a partially clear sky with a layer of thick blanket of snow in front of his view it looks as if more snow is to come later on tonight, he looked at his watch and it was near noon time, so he decided to get lunch. Jim got ready and got dressed and walked to his car he looked to his neighbor's house to see if the detective was still there, he had just went inside their house so he got in his car and headed off to town. As he drove off, what he not noticed was the dead looking lady standing in the middle of the street, her pitch black eyes peering through him as he drove off. The weather was ready to bring more snow, the clouds are getting thicker and darker, and the weather is getting colder. During that time, Detective Smith was finishing up on questions he had. According to Jims neighbors, loud thumps can be heard before and after their dog disappearance, they showed the detective where the dog was kept the chain is broken and the kind of dog it was, a special breed, a two hundred pound dog, to guard the family and loyal and playful with his kids, and the chain looks as if someone pulled it with a car to break it. Also some very heavy footprint impressions were found and are unusually big. Detective Smith has casts of the print made. One of the kids residing in the house asked the detective "Why make casts, it's a missing dog, not a person, right?" at that the detective told the kid "Well, that big foot cast may be of the same one who took your dog and put a man in the hospital and injured your neighbor," A surprise look on the kids face is all that was left. As Jim was getting lunch, he received a phone call, from his friend's professor David Sunnor, Jim answers the phone, and the professor says "Jim, is this you?," Jim answers "Yes, this is me, who's this?" then he answers "Hi, this is Professor David Sunnor, we spoke earlier with your friend Jeff." Then Jim said with delight "Oh yes! Yes how are you sir?" 'I'm doing great, thank you, hey, I have a friend that would like to meet you, he is a specialist, in linguistics, I showed him your photos of the emblem and he said he must speak with you at once, so he's coming tomorrow." "Ok, sure that will be fine, um where do we meet, when?" Jim asked. Then the professor said "He wants a place, where we all can sit down, a little privacy, say the library, they have private conference rooms say, before noon tomorrow." Jim said "That will be fine." "Ok then, well look forward to seeing you, and hearing what he has to say." The professor said. The arrival of a specialist of linguistics had got his mind off of the troubles he was having to a certain degree, now he was exited and anxious to meet someone who may know how to decipher the inscriptions. As he was heading home, he happens to catch something in the corner of his eye. It was the dead looking woman who is now after him. He quickly turned around, and looked in the mirror and saw nothing. He was very certain of what he saw so he turned around and went back slowly to look, and found nothing. To his satisfaction he turned around and headed back to his house. By then it was late afternoon, and nightfall is soon to follow. He headed back, parked his car then he went inside to eat is meal. At the same time, in the police station Detective James Smith was looking at his cases and his castings after looking at his gatherings he decided to go to the cemetery. He took an officer with him. They both were on rout to the cemetery they just arrived on site at the entrance they were driving until they ran into that strange lady Jim had encountered earlier days ago, and again in the library. She seemed scared. And almost run over by the officer and detective. They pulled over and said "Ma'am could you please got off the street and on the sidewalk." She was so scared she could hardly talk, finally they calm her down, she got her composure and said "I, I, I saw an evil in those back mausoleums." Both the detective and officer looked at each other. And she continued "Something not right here, this place is supposed to be empty lifeless peaceful, no not this place." The detective told the lady "Ma'am what are you talking about?" then the lady pointed at the back mausoleums. The very back one, the one made of black marble. Then she said "I have to go, I've got to get out of here." And then she took off running. The detective and officer drove a little further to the end of the road that ended parallel with the end of the cemetery. There they can see the mausoleums. They looked at each other then they got off then they started walking in the cemetery. They did not have a lot of time, daylight was running out. After a short walk they arrived to the back location of the cemetery, it was a site to behold rows of mausoleums public and private belonging to wealthy families and important individuals. There was one in particular, a black marbled one. There is something about it that made it unusual the style the appearance as if something is being kept from coming out. As they waked around the detective saw the side of the fence where the damage is, it is his good surmise that this is the spot where Jason was hit pretty hard. The bars that are bend outwards as if something came out of the building and hit him. This got even more puzzling to the detective, what would someone be doing inside the gate, possibly inside the building? So, the detective decided to enter the gate and look for any signs of recent disturbances in or out of the building that would suggest tampering or otherwise entering this building. Time was not on their side. The sun was rapidly starting to set. So the detective pulled out his camera and with help from the officer they gathered as much as they could. The detective took photos as the police officer collected tangible evidence, there was one piece of evidence the officer found it was a piece of black rag, it was collected, for analysis. And the detective was taken pictures and was looking at the front door, and it showed recent signs of disturbances it has been opened, but not from the outside, there is no force entry signs there, and then he notice something missing from the front of the building, something that use to be there. A decorative piece or crest or emblem, whatever it was its missing, it's showing signs of recent removal. He was about to touch one of the emblems until he heard an awful scream coming from on top of the building, he looked up and too much of his surprise the same big menacing bird that Jim saw is also screaming at them. His appearance was evil. Finally there was no light left, so both the detective and officer left to the car still looking at the big bird watching them they go into their car and headed back to the station. As they drove back the detective asked the officer "Did you see that big ugly mean looking bird, that looks as if can rip things to shreds." The detective said that bird, I don't think it's from this country, meaning, it's bigger than a condor, maybe meaner it's not indigenous to this part of the country. As they got closer to the station, the detective remembered the damage to Jim's car, and Jim saying it was done by a big bird. A sense a chill sent through the detective, all the things Jim has been showing him has been true, except the elusive skeleton figure they both Jim and Jason spoke of. And the bars of the fence made of old rod iron surrounding the mausoleum, those bars do not bent easy, as a matter of fact some great force has to hit for those bars to bend like that. When they arrived at the station, the detective took the evidence collected and, brought them to the crime lab for analysis. As the detective sat in his office, he was putting all his material together concerning the case involving Jim and Jason. Night fall has already set in, and at Jim's house he is settling and getting ready for bed, so far that he has not seen today, nothing out of the ordinary has happened except that glace. That was all about to change, as Jim was at his kitchen looking for a drink to take to bed with him, he could hardly hear at first but gradually getting louder wicked laughing coming from outside his kitchen window. It was the most horrific laugh ever heard, a laugh as if mocking your demise to come soon, a laugh that meant to shake things up, a sinister laugh getting louder and louder, he looked outside his window and saw the a horrific sight of a woman who looks long sense dead, dried and decaying looking at him laughing. Jim was frozen out of fear as the laughing continued. The laughing started comical and ended up in mockery. Then the laughing stopped, she stood looking at him still smiling then she started to cry horribly first a sympathetic cry progressing to an angry in rage cry. She was screaming at him she started to punch the window softly then progress ably harder until the window broke. Breaking the window she cut her hand something was bleeding, after a short while she stopped punching and screaming. She just stood there looking at him, with her deep black eyes then without warning she began to growl, an unearthly growl. Then she left from the window site. When it seems that she left, Jim called the detective. The detective said he'll be over as soon as he can. It seem to take forever for the detective to arrive at Jims house, he finally did as he approached his house Jim was waiting for him outside to show him what had just happened. The dead woman who was laughing at him and her breaking the window the detective saw the broken window, and looking at the window the detective asked Jim, "Aren't those windows double plain glass, and hard to break?" looking in disbelief still Jim said "Yes, they are." Then something caught Jim's eye, as well as the detectives. As Jim started to reach for the broken window the detective said "Here I got it, I'll get it." The detective retrieve what seemed to be a piece of old flesh with old cloth and put in a small plastic bag. Undoubted the detective said "You're in a pretty messed up position,

in all my years in my career have I have never come across this, I mean
dead things are after you." As he was walking to his car he turned
around and asked Jim "Would you like to go sleep at the station, they
have comfortable couches there in the lounge?" shaking his head Jim
said "No, I'll be fine." Then the detective said "Ok, suit yourself." Then
he drove off. After the detective left, Jim went inside to put a plastic
film on the broken window, so no cold will enter. Satisfied that the
window is sealed him then heads to his bedroom, he changed his mind
about the drink. As he started to turn to walk towards his bedroom,
he froze, right in front of him, there is the dead looking woman
looking right at him in the eyes with only a low tone growl. Trying to
back up, Jim was looking for an escape from being trapped in the
kitchen, with only the table between him and the woman. They circled
around the table twice, finally they stopped then with anger or
frustration the lady with one chop from her arm, she broke the table in
two this was no small table, and it was a heavy thick wood table not
easily broken. With fear Jim jumped back wards falling to the ground,
only to have the woman walk over to him and pick him up and hold
him close to her face about maybe a foot distant from each other's
face. This dead lady is around six foot all, Jim is less than six foot tall,
and so she towers over him a few inches, and has him picked off the
floor to her sight level. Jim struggled to break free, as he barely did and
ran towards his room. Just as soon as he did the woman did also. She
pushed him hard to his bed, as he slammed to his bed she got on top
of the bed walking on it with him still panting yelling and screaming
at her. Finally she stopped, kneeled on top of him, and continued to
look at him with a low tone growl and let one more horrific scream
that Jim fainted, leaving him out for the rest of the night. As daybreak
arrives Jim was awoken by, the phone ringing. He jumps out of bed
looking all over for the woman, and found nobody. Still shaking Jim
got up to answer the phone, it is his friend Jeff. Struggling to say
anything Jim finally says "He, he, hello." Then his friend Jeff says "Jim,
where are you, the professor is here along with his friend, who says he
needs so see you now, it's the upmost importance he speaks with you."
Jim still trying to struggle with his recent episode with the dead
woman intrusion says, "Give a little time I didn't set the alarm." At
that Jeff told him "Alright, were going to be at the library, in one of

the private rooms, well see you there." "Ok." Jim said. Jim got ready as soon as he could, and rushed to get to the library, he did not dare tell them about what has happened to him last night, for he had enough trouble as it is. As he stepped out the weather again was overcast, the sun's rays are blocked and snow is starting to fall. As he backed up to drive off he saw that dead woman again, in his rearview mirror, he stopped, and stayed looking at her all she did is stood there looking at him, with a semi evil grin. At that Jim had an idea, he put the car in reverse, and slammed the gas, hoping to ram her. She was much too quick to be hit, she moved to a side quickly, and then Jim stopped. When he stopped, his window was almost parallel to where she is standing, and Jim started to take off, until he noticed a big black dog in front of him, not on the road, but on the hood of his car. This dog is bigger than the neighbor's dog, and vicious. He is big in size at least one time bigger than his neighbor's dog, black in color of fur, and red evil glowing eyes, and the biggest sharpest teeth ever seen. He barks seemed to be amplified, every time he barked Jim's ears ached with fear. The dog started with his big paws scratching the windshield of his car. This is a very strong dog, with his big paws he was hitting the glass and making round spider web like cracks on the windshield and with his nails stars as well making deep scratches as the big bird did before, and biting the trim off the windshield. Jim put the car in drive and stepped on the gas causing the dog to off balance, falling off the hood of his car, the dog landed on all four legs. As he started take off the dog started to run after Jim in his car biting his side mirror off, at that Jim yelled in panic. The dog went back to the lady at her side with the mirror still in his mouth dropping the mirror near her legs as Jim was driving franticly to meet his friend at the library, on his way he almost wrecked into another car, but narrowly escaped. Jim finally arrived at the library, still shaken up, more than ever, but hesitant to say anything to anybody about it. As he walked in the library, one of the librarians Cindy said to him pointing to the back side rooms "Oh Jim, hi, hey there over there in that room waiting for you." "Thanks Cindy. "Jim said. With much nervousness, and anticipation, Jim started to walk in on one hand, as an archeologist, he wanted to know and learn, about things of old. On the other, he kind of now is finding out something's are meant to be left alone, undisturbed. His gut feelings are mixed, for what he's about to find out. He walks in all in the room stands up, his friend, the professor, and now the specialist who wanted to see him very much. "Hey there he is." Jeff Said. Then Jeff said to the professor "I believe you've already met Jim," nodding the professor shook his hand, then Jim and Jeff turned to the specialist and said and Jeff said Jim this is "Mr. Brandon Stewarts, now Mr. Stewarts is a highly respected linguists and historian who is in his who is also from Europe Jim then shook hands with Jim. As he shakes his hands with Mr. Stewarts, he noticed Jim's hands trembling and cold, Jim knows why he's shaking and it's not because of the cold weather. Coincidently, Mr. Stewarts thinks the same because of the news he has to tell him of his discovery is grim. As they all sit down Mr. Stewarts asks Jim, "Why are you shaking? It's not because of the cold weather is it?" trying to put on a smile Jim says "Yes." Looking at Jim as if he was not really telling the truth, he goes on to start telling Jim of his find. Mr. Stewarts starts by saying to Jim and Jeff "Of course you all know why I'm here, the professor who showed me some photos of your find, and couldn't decipher, the inscription, right?" they all nodded. Mr. Stewarts looked at everyone in the room, and proceeded to say" These inscriptions come from Europe, and are from a unknown secrete society group of hunters, not ordinary hunters, but hunters of evil, and the keepers of their captures, meaning in simple jailers and executers." Jim, Jeff and the professor all looked at one another in amazement. Then Mr. Stewarts said "This is seal saying he who breaks the seal is doomed for all eternity." As he continued he went on to say "The other emblems are seals also preventing an outburst of evil from pouring out, with the side saying for all time ye who is in this keeps is to be kept for all time, no breaking seal will keep this sure." As Mr. Stewarts continues a deep concern grows in Jim and is starting to eat him with in, for he knows now he broke the seal causing those god awful things to come out. Mr. Stewarts continues to say "The top emblem says to the trespasser, if you remove the seal, it empowers the kept to go after only the one who removes the seal and any who ye gets close." Then Mr. Stewarts says in simple it limits the ability for the ones inside to do more than they have to." Then Jim sunk in his seat, and then Mr. Stewarts turned to him and said "Young man, the seal you have in this photo is a seal that has been removed, and that's why I'm here, to warn you of coming consequences," This is the part where Jim has dreaded to hear in the back of his mind, after all has happened in the past few days. Mr. Stewarts pulled out a thick book that looked very old and has the very same emblems as did the museums bound in leather and metal trim presumably the same metal used as the emblems of the mausoleums. He looked at everyone and especially at Jim, and told them "I come from Europe, not going to say exact where but that I will say, now, Jim, you removed this emblem or should I say seal, right." Looking at him Jim said with a lump in his throat "Yes." Then he opened it, then flipped through some pages and stopped, and then he slides the book to Jim, and asked him, "Did you see this figure at first?" Jim then slid the book close to him and looked at the picture, and sure enough it is the picture of the big bird, evil and menacing in a picture as is in life. The picture is that of a hand drawing portrait of them just in black and white. Jim's eyes got big and said with a crackling voice "Yes." Mr. Stewarts just stayed looking at him for a short while and then he said "It's the eye of the evil entities whatever they want to know, or want to know where it is, it will seek it out." Then Mr. Stewarts said "You were seen removing that seal by the eyes of those in kept, and more than likely it squawked at you, meaning it was warning you." Then Mr. Stewarts then gestured for the book back, Jim handed the book back then he started to turn more pages and then stopped and handed him the book with the pages opened and asked him "Now look, did you see this thing next?" Jim then looked at the pages where the book was opened and to his fears coming true by the minute, he saw the picture of the sickle less death figure. With a petrified look on his face he said "Yes." Then Mr. Stewarts had a long stare at him. There was an eerie silence in the room, now Jeff and possibly the professor didn't believe them at first but now their doubts are fading away by the minute. Then Mr. Stewarts gestures the book his way, then Jim hands it to him, then he said as he flipped the page this is his true form, and he gives him back the book and Jim looks at it for about a minute, then gives the book back then, he tells Jim, "He was the silent stealthy killer, he killed people in their sleep in their home, anywhere without being seen." Jims breathing continues to breath heavier by the minute. Then Mr. Stewarts turns the pages and stops and asks Jim, "Did you see, this one afterwards?" hesitant Jim had the book sided to him, and he looked and sure enough it is the tall heavy walking skeleton with a long black weathered trench coat. Jim had a look of he is doomed and he said "Yes." Then taking back the book Mr. Stewarts said "He is the muscle of the bunch, the enforcer, the messenger of doom, he is also the bounty hunter and goes after anyone who does wrong to their own." Then he turned a page and showed him a picture of his former self, a strong tall big man, the kind to be reckoned with." Then he turned the pages and stopped, and looked at Jim for a while, then Jim looked back as if something was terribly wrong, then he again slide the book over to Jim and asked "Did you see this one next?" as Jim looked at the photo, his blood ran cold. It was the picture of the dead looking lady, not wanting to look at Mr. Stewarts, Jim says with a low tone "Yes." Then taking back the book he turned another page then showed him another picture of her in her true form. Then he said to Jim "She is a woman who is tall thin feminine a trapper who lures men and others into their demise she is the front face of the group." Then he looked at Jim and then he said "Now did you see this last one." Handing the book with the pages turned to the last figure he saw today and that is the big black dog. He said "Yes." Then Mr. Stewarts said he is the watcher during their time of rest, he watches over them, and he assists in hunting and capturing their victims sometimes mauling them." After telling Jim this, he closed the book and then he told him, "My friend, it appears you have been targeted, once you have seen all these evil entities, it's too late, you are to be taken to the darkness." At that Jim got up fast and walked off fast. Still stunned of what just went on, Jeff and the professor asked "What do you mean he's doomed?" at that Mr. Stewarts said "I know a lot about history, and this right here, is part of a history that is not known openly to the rest of the world." "As for the keepers, there is little known about them, of what I do know are they having unusual long lives, how many, I don't know, their identity, neither," he added. Then he pulled out the book again opened it and showed them a picture of the keepers, a man with father his five sons and two daughters. During the time Jim ran out of the library, detective Smith is putting together pieces of his case he went to the police vault to the cold case files. All of these happening events are not making sense to him, he had a feeling there was an occurrence once before. To purge his suspicion the detective started to look. At the same time him headed to his house and got the emblem and headed back to the cemetery in hopes to advert his doom by putting back the emblem where he took it from. As he headed back to the cemetery he noticed nothing out of the ordinary, no evil entity following or watching him or after him, nothing. The snow was getting heavier by the minute, making a little hard to see and drive, finally he arrived. When he got down, he looked around for anything that would suggest he was about to encounter trouble. And nothing, so he proceeded to the back of the cemetery where the mausoleum is at, the gate is mysteriously opened, which it was not before, but he paid it no mind, he was on a mission to put it back and not come back, ever. So he proceeded to the building and placed the emblem on where he had pried it off, he tried to work it on back. But no matter how or what he tried nothing, the emblem just kept falling off to the ground. He kept picking it back up and tried to jar it to place, and nothing, it just fell. By this time he was getting desperate, he got pieces of wood for shims and picking up a rock he tapped it back leaving it snugged. To his satisfaction, he saw it did not fall off so he went off back to his house, but this time he was going to move out of this town and leave it, move elsewhere far, far away from this place, especially this latest scary events. He drove off speeding towards his home and when he arrived he started packing only clothing and personal belongings. His thinking is the farther the better, and has a clean start and leave things alone. Because of his curiosity, it got him in a world of trouble, or should he say in another worldly trouble. He finished packing, and locked his door and would not look outside nor answer his phone, for he became a recluse. Though out the day his phone rang, the door knocked and he did not answered, as night fall came he did not have any lights on, for he was afraid it would attract some unwanted attention from unwanted company. Especially from his newly acquired terror that seems to have a taste for him. As the night progressed, he sat still in the dark ever so quiet, his solitude was shattered by a phone call that he simply ignored and silenced, and he did not even want anything to be heard from his house to suggest he was home. For again, he did not want no unwelcomes scary visitors. When the phone calls stopped it was quiet one more, so quiet its loud quiet. The snow falling was filtering the noise from the city, it was quiet. So in the dark he sat in the quiet waiting for at least daylight to make his move, by the time those things move or decide to look for him, he'll be long gone. His car can take him a far distance in a shot while. At the same time Jim was sitting in the dark, the detective was still in the cold case vault looking in the cold cases. As he was about to call it the day he noticed a very old envelope, labeled unsolved case number 1870, he took as the 1870 was the year that took place. He opened the envelope case and sat down in a chair with a table in the room. He began to look through it, and much to his amazement in his reading the investigating officer's report it had similar situations on assaults strange siting's and disappearances, much like the case he has. The detective got up and took the old case with him and went to his office, and proceeded to read further. During his reading the descriptions of the assailants are strikingly similar to the ones he has in his case he's working on. So, he started to compare notes and he concluded that the victims as Jim did had, in his possession of something that did not belong to him. And like the victim before him he too was assaulted and finally disappeared without a trace. During his assaults he started to develop drawbacks from everyone, he noticed that on Jim, he was starting to not be as opened as he used to. Convened Jim has something not belonging to him that is bringing him this calamity, he decides he's going to Jim's house and talking to him about what he has in his possession. He gets to his car starts it, but he couldn't go far, the snow was blinding, it was too thick for driving. So goes back calls Jim and no answer so he is going to Jim's house first thing in the morning, or when he had the chance weather and conditions permitting. He had to stay in the station that night. Sense he was not going anywhere tonight he did more looking and reading into the case and testimonials of witnesses. The case was more than a hundred years old. He wrote the names of witnesses and the officer's names and looked up their names, in the stations computer in hoping he can find surviving relatives or someone in the family who may have passed down stories or facts or proofs. Who may have been told or have some kind of information that would help his case and to finally put a name to the illusive faces that do the assaulting and abducting. The detective finally made a few connections, he happens to locate four descendants of the people involved in the case back then. And fortunately two of them lived near by the station so on foot the detective went to find out what they knew. As the detective went to contact these relatives, Jim was at home, in the dark and real quiet. Jim was inside siting down in a fettle position against the front door as he was sitting down he could hear an eerie silence and it was total darkness inside his house, except the pale light coming from the skies with the moon somewhat peering through, the snow has stopped falling. As he was sitting in the dark his silence was broken by a scratching noise coming from outside his house. As he listened with much freight he came soon to realize it was the tree outside rubbing against the house, there was a light wind outside. All throughout the night he sat there, in the dark waiting quiet. The detective arrived at the first person on his list it was a great, great grandson of the officer who worked on the case he now has reading. He knocked as he waited, the door opened, and an older gentleman answered "May I help you?" he asked, the detective introduced himself to him, and the let gentleman him in. As they sat down in the living room, the gentleman attended the fireplace by putting more wood to burn. And then he asked the detective "How can I help you?" Then the detective asked him" What do you know about your great, great, father? Who worked as an officer?" as he picked at the fire place he said "My great, great, grandfather retired after his last case, it plagued him." Looking at him the detective asked him, "Is it about strange siting's assaults, and disappearances?" He stood still for a moment looked at the detective and asked him "How did you know that?" looking at him, the detective said to him "Something like that, as a matter of fact a lot like that is happening." Then looking at the detective he said" Oh my god" Then he got up and walked off, and as he did he turned to the detective and said "I'll be right back, I have something you might want to look at." And then he walked off to the hall way of his house. The detective waited in anticipation and then what it seems was going to be a long time, he comes out. "Here detective, this might be of help to you, I hope." It was an old folder a dark brown folder that contained great grandfather's notes concerning the case. As he looked through it he had drawings, sketches of witness's descriptions of the assailants. He was stunned the drawings are detailed. As he looked up he asked "Do you mind if I borrow this for a little while?" looking at him with a sense of helpfulness he said "Sure go ahead" The detective thanked him for his contribution in his case and off to the next place he'll go to before its late in the evening. During that time of the detective going to the second and last stop for the night, Jim was already started to get sleepy, but too much afraid to sleep. Jim is afraid to sleep and to be wakening up to a horrible predicament as he has before, but still after the visit with the specialist, he had the feeling of hopelessness in him as if his days are numbered, and a sense of uncertainty is in. Finally he fell asleep lying down on the floor in a fettle position curled up. He was fast asleep, he kept having not bad dreams but bad scenes in his mind that happened plating over and over again, with that he kept waking up. Then looking around, looking realizing he's at his house and he eases up a little then he stays awake then eventually falls back asleep. Meanwhile The detective finally arrives in his final stop on his list, he knocks, an older lady answers it, and asks" Yes, can I help you?" Showing his badge to her, he identifies himself to her and asks if he can come in to ask some questions. She goes ahead and lets him in, and he proceeds to ask. He first asks about her great, great, grandmother and if she hasn't told her any stories of unusual things she might have seen when she was small. Then they both sat down in her living room, and she thought for a short while, then she said "My grandmother told me a long time ago, her grandmother spoke to her when she was a child of something she once saw that scared her, that, her great grandfather encountered it when his friend was scared out of his mind and was hurt real bad he needed a doctor, as his friend ran to my grandfather for help, my grandfather put him inside of our house and called the boys, meaning his sons nephews, brothers, they armed themselves, as the girls try to help grandfathers friend they could hear as my great-grandmother describes it as heavier than a big horse steps coming in the night. But when that thing came, it looked like bones of death, and great-grandfather and everyone outside tried to stop it but threw everyone back very far and got your grandfathers friend and took him away. Nothing, nothing could stop it, no matter how many times they shot at it, it took him away, you could hear him scream and yell as he was carried away into the night never to be seen or heard from again." Then the detective asked "Did your great grandmother, drew or had pictures of this thing to the police?" at that she said "Hold on." At that she walked off and grabbed an old book and handed it to the detective, and said "We had our own artist in our family, and when great grandfather, and grandmother told him everything he drew this." Much to the detective amazement it was very similar to the drawings of the first one that he had. Then the detective said "Thank you for your time ma'am." As he walked through the front door the, lady asked, "Excuse me for asking, but why are interested in a very old story and drawing?" at that he turned and said "Legends never die, I guess." At that he turned to her and said "I have a few witnesses that saw your scary thing a couple of days ago." Then he walked off and then he walked to the precinct to finish up for the day. As the night slowly progressed the detective had a list of things to do, one of them is to talk to Jim of a possible object that was taken from its place that may have contribute to his dilemma. Because the snow prevented the detective from going to Jim's house, he would wait for daybreak to do so, in the meantime hell sleep at the precinct. After what it seemed to be a long night and Jim had the most uncomfortable night of sleep he's ever had, morning has broken the night sky, Jim was still uncertain to what to think anymore, too afraid to move and so glad to see the sun come up. The snow had stopped falling sometime during the night. It is a sunny clear morning and Jim is so relieved to live through the night. As he walked through the house, he made sure of no intrusions or leftover surprises. Satisfied with no surprises left, he opened the front door let the bright daylight in to brighten the darken house. As he walked outside he saw the bright sun, the clean white now that has yet to be stepped on. He took as the undisturbed snow as a good sign. As he stepped out to his front porch, he felt a hard object under his foot. As he looked down to his foot and when he saw it, he immediately closed the door fast and locked the door. To his shocking it is the emblem. One of those things had come to his house during the snow and placed it on his front porch. This is an indication that it's too late, they are coming for him, when he doesn't know, how he doesn't know, which one, he doesn't know either, and too afraid to think of which one it would come or if it would be all of them. He couldn't help but recall back the conversation he had at the library of his fate already sealed and he's doomed. This somewhat altered his plans to leave town he had to pick the right time to do what he intended to do, but now at different time. As the morning went by phone call after phone call not answered. Now any little thing bothers him. Now the slightest movements the slightest anything will make him jump. Morning was progressing to noon, and now the detective saw the ice had melted enough to allow him to go to Jim's place to have a talk to him. At that time, Jim decides to take off to the cemetery, to put back the emblem once and for all, and then skip town. On his way he noticed the sky's beginning to darken up and the snow is coming, so he decides to move before the snow closes the highways to where he's going to leave. On his way he went to the cemetery to put back the emblem, by the time he arrived, the snow already started to get heavy falling. As he was going to get off, he all of a sudden noticed a darkness in front of him, it was the death figure without the sickle, he froze with fear, trying to turn on the ignition he couldn't, he looked in the rearview mirror and to his already fear sees the tall walking skeleton then to his side the dead woman looking at him with her sinister grin. He is surrounded by pure terror and now, has to escape for dear life as he turned on his car, he shift it on drive and pressed the gas all it would go, the car took off peeling out missing the sickle less death figure, going uncontrollably and with no traction he sunk into a soft muddy patch of dirt, there his shifting his car drive and reverse proved useless, it only sunk it deeper in the mud. At that he saw them vastly approaching him, he tried to get out and run, but they proved too quick. Suddenly the passenger door flew off the car with such force it flew across the street. Then instantly the inside of his car was filled with suffocating darkness, and with Jim screaming and hollering trying to break free, with no avail to his efforts. Then darkness leaving the inside the car dragging Jim with it, still trying to hold on, but the strength of the one taken him is much more stronger. Then in the cold glooming snowing darken day Jim is being taken to his demise. The tall heavy walking skeleton with the tall hat is carrying him in one hand while Jim is kicking and wiggling trying to shake free begging it to let him go. Down to the end of the cemetery with Jims cry's, yelling, begging for his life can be heard as they are heading towards the mausoleum fading. When they get close to the mausoleum, the death figure and the dead lady wait, opening the gate they go through and the doors of the mausoleum are opened and all go through with Jim taken with them still struggling to break free. Deep in the darkness they went. Before the door to the mausoleum closes a hand slaps the emblem back on the side of the door opening of the mausoleum with a strong force, it sparks into place. Then the door closes with the screams and yells of Jims fading to a quiet snowy wind. At that time the detective was already driving up to the cemetery with two squad cars, running out with their guns pulled out, after going to Jim's house and not finding him there and answering to a police call from a nearby residence of reported a car reckless driving hysterical screaming. They spend a considerable time looking all they found is Jim's car sunk in mud with the door ripped off, and found across the street. The detective is quite certain it is Jim's car, because of the damage marks on top of the car he was shown by Jim. They make their way back to the cemetery to see if they can find more evidence, al they found is the missing emblem in place still smoking. As the detective and the officers looked they all put their guns back in their holsters. As they looked at the mausoleum it was as quiet as it was before nothing except an eerie silence. The detective has a disappointed look on his face, as if he could have prevented it look. As they headed back to the cars the detective turned around to have a last look, then he turned around and started to walk. The snow is falling and a little wind is picking up, and at that time as the detective was walking through the wind blowing, and he thought he heard a weak yell for help. He stopped, and listened again closely, and nothing else was heard. After a short while he stopped listening and went on. The detective went back to the precinct to complete his investigation on his case, but there was one more person he needed to visit, and that was Jason who is in the hospital. As he arrived Jason had already been moved from his room, the detective found his room and went in to visit him. When he walked in Jason asked "did you find the attacker?" then the detective said "Well before I do, I have questions of my own I need to know." Looking at the detective, Jason then said "ok" Then the detective pulled a chair and sat on it backwards with the back facing Jason. And then he asked "What were you doing in the cemetery when your attacker attacked you?" Jason said "I was walking reading stones." Then the detective asked "Did you happen to be at the back of the cemetery, near the mausoleums?" and then Jason said "Yes, reading

the older stones, and looking at the family names on the mausoleums."
Looking at him the detective asked" What were you doing and where
were you when your attacker attacked you?" Then Jason said" I was
reading stones, then the door to the mausoleum was opened, and I was
trying to take a better look to see if I could see inside, and then out of
what it seems to be the mausoleum the skull face came out and hit
me." Then the detective asked did you take anything that belongs to
the mausoleums, like a trim an emblem something like that?" "No"
said Jason. Nodding the detective said "I've have some leads I'm
looking into." Smiling Jason said "Thank you detective. Smiling the
detective left his room to leave him to recover. He went back to the
station to finish up the last of his case. A short time after the detective
left Jason was sitting in his bed in his casts looking out the window
from his bed thinking and wondering about that thing that hit him
with a lot of force. As he was looking out the window it was getting
late in the evening, and nightfall is close, as he was looking he eye
caught something in the trees, he wasn't quite sure. As he stayed
looking at the tree trying to focus on what he thought was in it, then
as he was looking for a while he soon gave up, then he started to fall
asleep as he did and his eyes drifted to sleep. The thing that was in the
tree was looking at him through the window with its red glowing eyes,
it finally came into view, it is the big vulture, the same one that was
one that was on the top of the mausoleum. Still in the tree while it was
looking in the window Jason was in and soft growl was heard under
him, it is the big black dog, the same one that bit the mirror off of
Jim's car. Both are looking at the window that is into Jason's room in
the hospital. Jason did not take anything from the mausoleum nor did
he trespass, he did see something, he was not supposed to see, not by
any human for that matter. For this his life is uncertain, only time will
tell if he is destined to have the same fate as Jim, or be watched, or the
presents of those things are a mere warning to him? For how long? It is
uncertain. As time went by, Jason's wounds and broken body had
healed. And the news of Jims disappearance has fizzled, and now
beginning to become legend and folk lore. Jason's injury has long been
healed, however he's not the same, and he's somewhat limited to his
abilities and strengths. Ever since his encounter with the tall walking
skeleton he's been having memory relapse, visions and not to mention

the big flying vulture and big black dog, that he's been seeing on and off on occasion. Everywhere he's been, going, it seems as if those two has been following him. Meanwhile somewhere in Europe, there is a secret society of hunters, jailers who are residing is a private fortress, they live in the fortress to conceal their identity and their longevity life, no one really knows the true age of these of the secret society. One of them the eldest of the sons who is next in line is just like his father, has black markings and black hair and eye colors are black is watching TV, and is watching a, news special of an American town where a disappearance has taken place. As he watches TV, he, records the program to show his father, he feels its news worthy to his father as he watches notices he mausoleum, and the emblem, their emblem, they had put centuries ago to keep the condemned ones from roving about the face of the earth. As he watched he also learns of the unfortunate soul they took, into their keeps, for removing the seal, they are not allowed to take nor remove the emblem, because of the dire consequences. The part that caught his eye is that one of them, had put the emblem back themselves, only the hunters, jailers have the power to put it back or remove it without the condemned ones, uprising. Because of this, the big bird and the big dog are still lose and might be stalking, and possibly planning on hunting killing, hurting, another soul, who had not touched the seal. On this account he must inform the others of the news concerning the condemned ones in this now America. Looking at the TV he sees the mausoleum, and starts to remember the day their apprehension took place and the trial they had for their wicked ways, but because there was no proof of their activities, through common knowledge they were found guilty, and sentence to be executed and their remains be put away for all eternity. Sense these are not ordinary people they cannot die, so extra precaution and preparation was needed to put them in their keeps and have them there for all time, the seals mounted on the entrance of the mausoleum prevented them from escaping, but tampering with them will break the seal, but, the seals still had power to keep them at bay, and now it seems as if what the seals are design to do, failed. As his thoughts deepen he remembers the woman with the condemned ones, he a long time ago had a special relationship with her, and she used to be his lover. Going back through his feelings his, once love was crushed by the woman he once loved. She loved trickery, deceit, and loves to pray one helpless ones, he was put in a hard position, the woman he loved so dearly was nothing more than a heartless witch, and now he was to do his duty and had to what had to be done, her along with her clan clashed, a war took place, before the war started they, advised all people to hide in their houses, lights out until this fighting is done and justice is done. Unpleasant painful memories surfaced with in him. Before her execution she had told him so passionately she loved him so and had an undying love, and can never harm him nor put him under her trickery. And she gave him one last kiss before she and the others was executed, after burning their remains, his family knew they could not die easily, so their remains was to be locked away. He and his brothers took their remains and put them away. As he had her burned body, his heavy sad heart, placed her with care in her keeping. He then turns off the recorder ejects the recordings turns off the TV and heads back to the grandmasters quarters with the recording to inform his father, the leader of the hunters. The hunters, they are as the condemned not mortal, they are in fact almost of the same kind of race. They are tall the father having black beard well-kept trimmed and stands about eight foot tall and his weight not certain had a powerful muscular physic. And has unique characteristics markings on his skin like tattoos or some kind of birth or mark of rights. His sons, total of five are unique as their father they also have an immortal lifespan that also not quite as tall or strong as their father yet, but tall and strong nonetheless, and stand approximately seven foot tall. Each of the sons have a unique characteristics as their father does each has different hair color, and the markings from their bodies matches the color of their hair and eyes. The eldest son like his father, had black markings and the eyes color is black, the next to the oldest is the one with yellow markings and eye color, the following is the blue colored one, then the green one, then the red one, total of five sons. He also has two daughters, one dressed in black and has black markings as well but a little smaller for a woman, and the other is blond and has light markings on her skin like her sister but lighter. The daughters are at least six foot four, slender athletically built, and strong, and very beautiful. A family meeting is called, all in the family is gathered, father the sons and daughters. The gather in the library of the fortress, when all is seated the father whose mane is Lord DarkWar, is seated on his seat, looking at his eldest son, making gestures of he wanted to know why they are called together, and only in important occasions do they gather together. And the eldest son whose name is Ondor proceeds to speak looking at his father then the rest of the family saying" We have a breach of our captives they are out and found a way to get out." Looking at one another and low tone of speaking, then with a puzzling concern look on his face Lord DarkWar then asks "Son, Ondor, how do you know of this, and how do you know it's our captives who has escaped?" At that, Ondor played the recording of the program he recorded from the TV, as the recording was playing all the family was looking at the TV with utter silence, as the program was playing the mausoleum which they had built was in view and then the sketch artist drawings of the suppose suspects who were seen in connection with a disappearance of a town local a sort of mockery of the drawings was suggested, because of the far-fetched appearances of the suspects, and a survival of a horrendous attack in the cemetery who claimed of a big skull faced thing that injured him and a big bird and a big dog occasionally following him. Then the program went on to say of it could possibly be a hoax or a stunt to get attention, but the disappearance of a town local could not be explained away. A detective who handled the case would not answer nor comment on the details of the case or the investigation. As the recording finished playing utter silenced filled the room. Lord DarkWar said to Ondor, "Rewind to the drawings showed." Ondor rewind to the drawings and froze the picture and all looked at the drawings, to their amazement the drawings are of exact of the captives they have. Lord DarkWar then stood up and said to all his sons and daughters, "We need to go back to this place, to set things right, nobody had to be injured, I wish this meddler would not have broken the seal, his fate would of not been so dark." Then looking at his eldest son he said "Ondor, I'm placing you in charge of our transportation and flight arrangements." Nodding, Ondor then proceeded to make arrangements for the family to go to America to this town where their captives are, and deal with them. Then he turned to his sons in birth order the one with yellow who preceded next and said Ionor, "You are in charge of weaponry, we can't have any kind of arms in flight the humans will not accept that, once

41

in the country search for appropriate arsenal." Nodding Ionor left, then he turned to the next the blue colored one and said "Kion, you are in charge of scouting, once were at the Americas we need as much as Intel as we can get." Nodding Kion left. Then he turned to the next the green one and said "Ryoc, you are in charge of our accommodations, look for a place that suits best our reason for being there. Then Ryoc nodded then he left, then he turned to the next one and said to the last the last and the youngest of the brothers who is the red one, and said "Endor, you are in charge of communications, you will talk to everyone at the same time to know of their whereabouts, and their progress and report to me." Nodding Endor then left. Then the two daughters were left and asked "Father, what of us?" Looking at them, he then said "You (the one in black) Irina will look for this survivor of the attack, the one who spent a long time in the hospital, he may be the key to drawing them out," Then he turned to the lighter dressed one and said "Amara, you and your sister has to protect this young man from the condemned ones." They both nodded at their father then they all attended to their assigned duties. Meanwhile back at the Americas Jason who was still trying to adjust still to his injuries was walking from his house to the library, when he noticed the big flying bird, swooping over him. He then duct and looked up and saw the big bird was coming around again to try to attack him once more. He then ran as fast as he could, as fast as his Injured body could take him. As he was running he went to a dead halt, on his path of running, the big black dog was in front of him growling with those big sharp teeth and eerie glowing red eyes that seem to be peering through him. Then he heard the big bird land behind him, he turned around and saw the big bird, almost his height, with a very wide wingspan walking towards him, screeching and screaming at him. At that time the big dog had already started to growl and bark horrendously. Looking at both with fear he was breathing hard panicking, and just about to faint till, the dog jumped him grabbed his leg by his pant and started to drag him, he was crying for help and screaming, at the same time, the big bird was already gripping him with its claws and flying lifting up with the dog keeping him down, it had seen that Jason was doomed till the bird was hit by a heavy broomstick on the side and he let go and began to fight the male pedestrian and manage to take his broom away. At the same time, the dog that had him by the leg pants was also hit by another pedestrian with a crowbar. At that he let go and started to walk towards the other male pedestrian who hit him, growling and fixing to jump him till he saw a pickup truck coming his way fast to run him over. The dog moved and the truck missed at that both the dog and bird left Jason alone and went away, but will be back again to attempt to get him again. When the creatures left Jason got up from the ground and thanked the two gentlemen for helping him and the driver on the truck. All three came up to him and asked him if he was ok, he assured them he was. After gratitude they all went their separate ways. Jason then went to the library and stayed there till closing time. Jason was not only scared of just what happened but was also baffled, it's not every day an oversize bird and dog come after you. For several hours Jason was at the library pondering on what has just happened. Closing time arrived, and Jason did not want to go out, not after the recent scuffle he had. But he had no choice it was closing and he had to go, so he left outside looking around cautiously, to his relief he saw Detective James Smith waiting outside for him. He approached the detective and said "Thank god you're here." And the detective looked at him and said "Yes, so I've heard you had a bit of excitement to day, quite unusual excitement at that." Shaking his head he looked at the detective and said "I was minding my own business, till I was jumped, so to speak." Looking at Jason the detective saw his injuries deep scratches and deep puncture wounds on his top half and big rips on his pants. Then the detective said "Come on, I'll give you a lift home but first we got to take care of those wounds," Jason nodded, then they got into his car and went to the emergency room to tend to his injuries. After a lengthy time in the emergency room the detective asked Jason "So, I was told you were attacked by a big black dog and a big black bird? Is that so?" Jason then nodded, and said" yes" looking at him the detective said "Here we go again." As they both walked out the hospital, Jason asked the detective "Can you give me a lift home, I'm not so sure if I should go walking." Nodding the detective said "Good thinking." They both got in his car and the detective drove him to his place of residency an apartment complex. As Jason got off he waved at the detective and walked off, the detective decided to wait and see him go inside his place for piece of mind. Once he entered and closed his door the detective drove off. As the detective drove off he looked in his rearview mirror and something caught his eye, he turned around, to see what it was he thought he seen. As he approached his suspicion is correct, he sees the big bird and dog wondering around where Jason lives. Much to his amazement, it is just as Jim and Jason described them to be, very big and very menacing. The big bird is that vulture he saw he said is not from this country is from another part of the world, the unusual size, height wingspan appearances and color, what's more creepy is the glowing red eyes peering through as if it was going to devour its prey. The dog also all black very big as a matter of fact much bigger than Jims neighbor's dog. A very muscular dog almost as big as a small horse, and as the big bird it too has glowing red eyes peering. The detective now knew there is now solid evidence of these things that are running all over town has the potential to kill any human at will. He calls for back up to hunt these things before they take another human as they did Jim, he believes now that Jason might be next, after his recent attack. As he waited for back up to arrive, he attentively watched the two creatures roam about looking, this is the part where he hopes Jason doesn't come out. Finally his back up arrives it is four squad cars with eight officers. The detective flags them down and tell them of the situation going on. All officers including the detective surround the apartments with orders to shoot to kill the bird and the dog. As the detective is looking for either creature, he hears a couple of shots, and quickly goes where the shots are heard from. As he runs to the area he sees an officer cornered with the big dog looking at him, he then fired at the dog once more yelling at it to stay back, but the dog kept coming forward to the officer. The dog started to let out an eerie growl not normal as other dogs but very evil and menacing. The shots fired to the dog seems to have no effect on it, the detective also fires at it, as he shot the big dog, it ignored the shots coming from the detective it kept getting close to the officer, the detective called out on his radio for back up for the officer who is cornered as the dog gets closer the officers arrive at the corner where the one officer is trapped and fires shots at the dog, and without warning the big bird swoops out of nowhere and cuts deep gashes on the officers forcing them to retrieve and head for cover. The detective who is former military refused to retrieve and fired at the bird which seemed also to no effect on it. As the detective fired at the bird and the cornered officer fired at the dog the other officers who were not hurt bad resumed firing at the bird and dog. By then the entire people living in the apartments were aware of the trouble police is having and are scared. The detective found cover and reloaded his gun, and radioed animal control to the scene, when he got up to resume fire the big bird was waiting for him and flanked him face to face. At the same time the cornered officer was pounced on by the big dog. The officers were firing at the dog and bird, but with no avail the detective managed to get the big bird in a headlock as it tried to stab him with its big beak, but was in pain because of the claws scratching his feet and lower body and with its wings flapping fast, and it screaming horribly. The officer was totally defenseless with only his forearm blocking the dog's mouth from ripping him, still the dog biting and tearing away. With his free hand the officer put the gun in the dog's mouth and fired the last shots in his pistol. The shots seemed to have no effect, if any it only enraged the dog. During all this commotion taking place just outside his apartment Jason is looking out the window of his apartment and is scared, he knows those things are out to get him, and will stop at nothing. All that he has seen this night is testament of his coming demise. He can run, but he can't hide. All of a sudden both bird and dog stopped their attack, and left as if something called out to them, leaving the detective and officer with wounds there was no casualties, just injuries that required first aid. Both the detective and officer stayed the night for observation both acquired a high fever, from the deep wounds and the close encounter with the two creatures. The detective left the very next day, the officer, needed some surgery to fix the damage the dog had done. The detective went back to work, at the station filing reports and doing more investigating, something told him this is not over, and it is not an isolated incident. He went over the cases once more, remembering the incident that took place the other night, as he was looking he saw the drawings rendering of the creatures and their masters, they have been seen before. As his investigating progressed his eyes caught a drawing an eerie drawing at that, it is of the dog and bird attacking pedestrians, quite similar to the one that has happened to him and the officer the other night. Meanwhile arriving at the airport the hunters arrived, the father his five sons and two daughters, heading towards the town where Jim had been abducted and Jason has been assaulted and now the detective has his first scuffle with the evil creatures. Meanwhile they headed to their destiny in two vehicles', two large black SUV, with one trailer each black in color. The vehicles' both have tinted windows. All through the travels and their stops, of their destinations, people kept looking at them, and their features and their sizes. People knew just by looking at them, they are not from this part of the country nor the world for that matter. From the father and sons to the daughters their sheer sizes are an attraction, and their appearances the father, who is the biggest and tallest, and looks like a muscular giant, a force to be reckoned with. The sons not quite as big and tall as their father, but taller than most men, and their unusual appearances hair color eyes, and like their father, muscular built. The daughters, a real guy magnets, who appears to look like goddesses very elegant, tall, as some men a little under seven foot tall and strong than men, and surpassing beauty, their beauty is something to be behold but their size, and unusual strength makes them intimidating. Everywhere they went, not planned or desired, they draw crowds, their mission is to go in assist the situation, and take whatever necessary means to quell the problems and the effects it might have caused. Everywhere they go they always draw a crowd, from gas stations when there're putting fuel and servicing their vehicles, to restaurants where they stop and dine and take a break from long road trips, to hotels where they stay for the night, all their attempts to blend in with people in general has failed. Last thing they need is to bring attention to themselves and have a failed mission. So they decided to up their traveling and arrive earlier than they had planned, they took turns shifts driving till they arrived at their destination. Finally in a small old town older than the country itself, before the Alamo, before the revolution, an old town with a lot of old history, and a lot of dark history. Upon their arrival, the town seemed quiet calm quaint. They looked for a place to dine for the evening, and gather intelligence on the town's history and recent story's and folk lore's alike and to concoct their strategy they are to execute in to action. They all got off their vehicles and looked around it is still daytime hours with evening hours away. Each knew their specific job function, and attended to it. After getting situated they all gathered in a restaurant coincidently where

Jim last dinned before his disappearance. As they sit in their table waiting for a waitress to serve them, one of the girls Amara was overhearing a conversation on the other table about the disappearance of Jim and how Jason was badly injured and who was again attacked, but had it not been for a heavy duty truck driven to just about knock it out of the way he too would of disappeared. She soon learned this is Jim's friend, Jeff who was talking about Jim his friend's disappearances. She got up from her table from her family and said to them" I'll be back" Then she went to the other table where Jeff, and another gentleman who is name Eric were having their meal and having their conversation. She approached them and asked "Excuse me, May I sit with you two for a moment?" They both stopped talking and looked at each other and said" Ok" then she sat down with them, then they looked at her and Jeff said "Ma'am, is there anything I can help you with?" They both stayed looking at her marveling at her beauty and her unusual size, both men are less than six foot, and she on the other hand is over six foot. Very beautiful very elegant, very majestic, her size and beauty somewhat intimidated them. Then she said "I was overhearing your conversation, about this man Jim, is he a friend of yours?" Still looking at her in a trance she snapped her finger and said "Hello," And then Jeff said um uh yes he was." Then Jeff asked her "May I ask who are you, and why are you so interested in my friend's disappearance?" Smiling she said "I follow stories that are illusive and intriguing, and my name is Amara." Smiling she asked them, "Can you tell me everything about your friend Jim, pertaining to his disappearance, and finally tell me his place of residence." Then they proceeded to tell everything they knew about Jim, and his final days before he disappeared. From what he had discovered and took to study, to the scary frightening figures he saw just days after taking the emblem and his ever increasing erratic behavior, his attack in the cemetery that nearly left him permanently disabled, to his last known place of residence. Then the other man Jason, who was walking the cemetery and happens to see the door of the mausoleum opened and was trying to peer inside to see what was inside or who is inside. Then his sudden attack coming out from inside the mausoleum now he's being haunted by a big dog and a big bird, much like the one Jim described to the detective before he too and an officer was attacked by the same two evil creatures. Then she said with a smile "Thank you so much for your help." "My pleasure to help you ma'am." They both said at the same time. She then got up and waked off to the table where she came from and sat back down with her family. As she walked off, they couldn't help but look at her and marvel at her beauty and size, as she sat down with her family they also noticed they too are just as majestic as she is. They saw her talking to the rest of her family of what was said to her concerning the unfortunate victim and the other would be or is about to be the next victim. As she went on talking she went on telling her family of what she learned, one by one each one of their family members turned to look towards them. As they took turns looking their way, this was starting to make Jeff and Eric nervous, for they have never seen anything like what has happen in their town and now big people asking questions, all looking their way. In the time it took them both to get nervous close to scared, all but the father had looked their direction, it's possible they did not see their father, he remained seated. Much to their surprise the other daughter the one dressed in black Irina who was just as tall and beautiful as the light dressed one but dressed differently, but still beautiful nonetheless got up walked to their table and said to Jeff "I would like you to speak to my father, Lord DarkWar," Even more surprise, he agreed and nervously followed the beautiful Irina to their table, there Jeff saw their, father who is unusually big, more so than his children, looking at him. Then Lord DarkWar asked Jeff, "Have you seen these evil entities first hand, and have they seen you, and have you tampered with a seal?" Still looking at their father, he finally said "No sir." Smiling, then he told Jeff, "Then you're in no danger, only those who have any kind of close contact with them, or tamper with a seal, may have a possible attack." With little relief he nodded with acknowledgment, then he started to walk off, then he turned around, and asked him, "Is my friend Jim, doomed, for all time, like is there no hope for him at all?" looking at him, then he said "I am very sorry, but your friend has sealed his doom by removing what was not supposed to be remove at all." With a disappointing look on his face, Jeff sat back at his table, and begin to tell his friend Eric, their questions they had, then Amara the light colored dressed one with light colored hair said to Jeff, "Do you know where your friend, Jims place of residence is at?" looking at her Jeff said "Yes, I've visited him many times before, and dined and socialized with his at his place." Then she said "Ok, thank you, then she turned and walked to their table to their family. Jeff and Eric decided it was time to leave, and was about to go until the other daughter Irina walked over to them, and asked Jeff "Will you please go with us and show us, his place of residency?" Reluctant to cooperate, Jeff, stood up from his chair and was about to make up many excuses to as why he couldn't go with them, backing up he bumped into the eldest son Ondor, who was behind them, during his talking with Amara, Ondor walked past them and stood behind them from a distant, as soon as they got up he closed in on them. As Jeff turned to see who is behind him he looked and much to his surprise he saw an even taller person, than the women who was talking to them, looking at him Jeff "Oh, um, uh, a, who are you?", looking at them towering over them, standing seven foot tall, he said to Jeff "She's talking to you, it will be an honor having you come with us." Looking up at them all Jeff did is nod. They turned and said to Eric, "You have not seen nor come in contact with these we speak about, you're free to go, and stay out of their sight." So without hesitation, Eric left, and Jeff was taken by the light colored daughter Amara, he was to go with her. They all went to scout to different key places, they separated in two groups The first group the father the son in blue, green, red and the daughter in black, headed to the last place they left, over millenniums ago, the cemetery, the other went to Jims last known residence and last known locations. The first group arrived at the cemetery getting off their vehicle walking making their way cautiously back to the old part of the cemetery looking at the black mausoleum is the last thing they left, and leaving it sealed, and protected against any would be thief or agent of evil. As the approached, they noticed an eerie silence, an unusual silence they also noticed some activities of recent disturbance. The door which should have not been opened, has been opened, all the condemned ones are supposed to be inside with no way out, from the vulture, the dog, the death figure, the big tall walking skeleton, and the long dead looking lady. All with unusual powers and will use them to dispense their wicked ways to unfortunate victims, and consume them, or use them. After for a considerable time in the cemetery, Lord DarkWar decides it's time to deal with them once and for all, a battle will have to ensue to capture and destroy them once and for all. He will need bait to draw them out, in order to fully release the war that is to wage upon them. As they all waked off the cemetery they looked back to see if anything suspicious is or about to happen. As they left the cemetery they got on their vehicle, and waited a little longer to see if there was anything coming or going to the mausoleum, so far nothing. Meanwhile Jeff is in the other vehicle with the other group, with Amara going to Jims former place of residence, they finally arrived, his place is already has the windows boarded up and looks very dark, not a literal dark but an eerie feeling dark. A feeling as if evil has arrived and never left feeling. They stopped in their vehicle in front of Jim's house, and looked at it for quite some time. Then they decided to get down and look a little closer, upon looking around the neighbors just happened to notice them looking, Jeff saw the father of the neighbors looking at them from his front porch from his house. Jeff then approached him, and asked him "What do you know of this man, that once lived here?" At that the neighbor whose name is Kyle asked "Who are you? What are you doing here?, and why are you interested in my neighbor?" At that Jeff said I'm following stories." Then Kyle said "He was my neighbor for at least ten years, I had noticed erratic changes in him before he disappeared, and then before he disappeared our family dog had gone missing and was found in the cemetery." Jeff then asked him "What kind of erratic changes?" looking at him, Kyle said "He got paranoid, as if someone or something so evil so untold was after him." Then Kyle said to Jeff "As a matter of fact I, well my family and I have heard strange noised or sounds coming from his house of around his house, fear for my family I did not let them go outside, not even in their own back yard." Jeff asked Kyle "You said your family dog went missing and was found in the cemetery?" Kyle then said "Yes, as a matter of fact, he was barking profusely at my neighbor's house following real heavy footsteps, at least that's what we could make of the sound we were hearing, all we heard was his last barking then his what I can describe is his death grip, then silence." Jeff then asked him, "Did you call the police?" shaking his head he said no need, the detective was here the next day asking questions about my neighbor and our dog." Jeff then asked Kyle "Why your dog?" Kyle answered "because he was found dead in the cemetery." Jeff then asked Kyle "Did you see what was making the heavy footsteps?" Slowly shaking his head he said "Out of fear, I did not let my family look nor go outside for days, our dog is a special breed of dog, that is not easily overcome nor picked up." Jeff stood looking at Kyle and asking "Special breed?" Kyle then answered "I'm a certified special dog breeder, I do this for a living, and our dog had bruit size anywhere from one hundred fifty to two hundred pounds, strength, loyalty, and a family dog." Jeff asked him "Do you think that heavy stomping sound you heard might have been connected to the disappearance of your dog?" Nodding Kyle said "I don't want to sound superstitious but, I'm afraid so, that was no man outside stomping around." "Our fence was down, and we tied our dog to a body harness with a thick chain because of his size and strength, until we repaired the fence we had to keep him tied up." At that Kyle showed Jeff what he showed the detective the broken chain, the chain is the kind used to tow or pull other cars with, very heavy duty, and it was broken, as if it exceeded its pulling capacity. Jeff stayed looking at the broken chain with unbelief. Kyle said to him "No man can do this." As they walked back to the front of Kyle's house, Kyle said to Jeff "There is something else, my eldest son, was scared out of his wits when he saw a bigger dog than ours running after our neighbor's car." Jeff looking at him with a confirm of suspicion look asked him "Big dog?" Kyle answered back saying "That big dog my son saw, he showed me, we both saw it, it was easily twice the size of ours and not friendly it was solid black, with red glowing eyes, and an unearthly growl, it was chasing after my neighbor's car and bit the mirror off his car," Jeff looking at him repeated "Bit the mirror off the car." Kyle continued, "That dog from hell, is like no other dog I have seen, it could kill ours with no effort." When Kyle had just finished telling Jeff about the big black dog Amara had already walked behind him without him noticing her approaching him, them as soon as he was finished telling Jeff what he and his son had seen she said "The dog you are talking about is a dog of evil, a guard dog, an attack dog, whose sole purpose is to carry out its masters evil deeds," At that Kyle turned around and looked at Amara and was stunned at her appearance, not only is she beautiful, but she was very tall, elegant a goddess like. She towered over him, he is less than six foot, and she's over six foot. Still speechless he looks at her and finally says "I beg your pardon, who are you?" Smiling at him she says "We have come here to stop them." Kyle looking confused asking "We?" "Yes, we." Said Amara's brother, Ondor who was behind Kyle this time. Kyle turned around and looked even more stunned because her brother is even taller than she is. It is the eldest son, the one with black hair like his father towering over Kyle seven foot tall, even taller than his sister Amara. Ondor has an appearance of an athletic body builder with jet black hair, with beard the same color and markings on his body arms tattoo like that seem to move. Then what it seems to go out of nowhere the one on yellow hair appears from looking all over the outer house tells Ondor and Amara something did happened, but some time ago. Like his brother Ondor he too is athletically built and seven foot tall, with tattoo marking but only they are yellow like his hair and eyes. Kyle still stunned to what he's seeing, he's seen tall people before but not like this, never has he seen people that tall before, that towered over him seven foot. He can see pure godlike strength in them, a force to be reckoned with. There right before his very eyes, he sees three unusually tall individuals, two males the same height seven foot tall, and a female over six foot tall, about six foot four. Yet something from the inside of him tells him his life, nor his family's life is not is any kind of danger, looking at them he could tell they are on a mission to destroy what ever got his neighbor and killed his dog. To their satisfaction they finally started to head off from Jim's former place of residency, and headed to regroup with the others. As they got into their vehicles, Kyle was still looking at them, and marveling at their appearances, Amara turned back and walked back to Kyle and asked him for a favor, when she started to ask, Kyle's wife whose name is Wendy stepped out to see who Kyle was talking to, she too was astonished to see the size of Amara. Both were looking up at Amara as she asked them not to divulge to anybody of their coming to their neighbors place of residency. Both shook their heads at the same time still looking at her as she walked off towards the SUV, then they drove off to meet the rest of their family. Meanwhile at Jason's apartment, he finally builds up the nerve to get out of his apartment goes walking to a local coffee shop as walks he looks and hears around him carefully for any suspicious noise or sounds, as he walks he hears a vehicle approach from behind him, he turns around and it is Detective Smith now pulling up on the side of him. "You know, you might be attack again, by those things that might be following you, right?" The detective said to Jason. "Yes, but I needed to get out, for air, I am going to the coffee shop." Jason said. "I'll give you a lift, come on get in I could use coffee myself." The detective said. At that Jason got in and both headed both to the coffee shop. They both sat at the same table and enjoyed the fresh brewed cup of coffee. Jason said to detective Smith "I saw what happened, that night you dropped me off my apartment, and what I saw outside and I was terrified." looking at Jason, the detective said "That officer got mauled pretty good, by that dog from hell, he had to have emergency surgery, to save his arm, I'm not sure if he'll ever have full use of his arm again." Then Jason asked "And that big bird you were grappling with?" The detective looked at his chest and looked at Jason and said "That is the most biggest bird I have ever seen, he was at least your height, you are what, five foot six, and its wing span is about twelve foot give or take a foot. And pitch black feathers god awful red glowing eyes and smelled like it's been eating off of corpses." Jason is looking at the detective ever so attentively, and the detective continues "It was clawing at my chest, good thing I was wearing my vest, however it was clawing away at it, it has the biggest claws with razor sharp tips made to rip and tear, well it was ripping and tearing and ripping away at my vest, it managed to work its way around the vest and started to dig its way in me, the gun shots didn't seem to stop it, as the same for the dog," "Why did they just got up and leave." Jason asked. The detective said "I kept on thinking about, and it looks as if they were called off by someone or something." "Do you think it was bone face, you know the one that assaulted me?" looking at Jason the detective said "Possibly." Then the detective said to Jason "I don't think it's a good idea for you to go around by yourself in this town with those things running around, they did try to get you already before, unsuccessfully had it not been for intervene by other people, I would of have two disappearances instead of one, so if you need to go somewhere get public transportation or a trusted person for transport, ok." Nodding Jason said "Ok." Then the detective said "If you do see those things again around your apartment or following you, you call me do not delay." Nodding Jason said again "Ok." They finished their coffee and headed towards the cemetery, and then Jason asked the detective in a nervous tone "Why are we here?" Still driving the detective said "I need to check something out, you can stay in the can if you like, but if I have a question come out, don't worry I will not let anything happen to you." Still not convinced of his safety Jason hesitantly said "Ok." As the detective was driving around he noticed two big black SUV's parked at the cemetery each had a sizable trailer hitched behind them the same color as the vehicles themselves. He slowed down driving and he asked to Jason "I wonder who this is, at the cemetery, and what are they doing here?" "Your guess is as good as mine detective." Jason said. Still driving the detective decided to drive around the cemetery to get another angle and see if he can get a better view of the individuals near the end of the cemetery. What made the detective more interested is they are near the mausoleum where Jason was assaulted and the last cries for help were heard from Jim before his disappearance. The persons the detective was looking at are not recognizable however, he did recognize one, the shortest one in that group as a matter of fact, Jeff who was Jim's friend. The detective decided to park his car behind their SUV's and get off and ask them what they are doing there and why are they near the mausoleum. The detective got off, and said to Jason "I'll be back." Then he walked off to encounter the mystery persons in the cemetery. As he left Jason was feeling nervous by the minute, he couldn't help but wonder if the detective is going to face certain danger with those people who look tall and mysterious. As the detective walked inside the gates of the cemetery he felt a sense of nervousness but curious at the same time, he wanted to know who they are and what they are doing at the mausoleum. As he was approaching closer to them he stopped and looked for a while at all of them and studied them and their appearance and judging by Jeff standing next to them their size, he could estimate the females are his height and the males are taller, and the unusually tall one has to be the leader or the authority figure. He stars to walk towards them again as he gets closer they one by one notice him getting closer to them as he gets to their proximity Irina the dark dressed daughter approached him and begins to ask him "What do you know of this building recent activities, has it been disturbed, entered, had anything come out of it?" looking at her with such amazement never has he seen a woman his height and very beautiful elegant and athletically built goddess like, she is dressed in black. He is mesmerized my appearance and looks for a while then after a while she says with a smile "Hello." Still a little mesmerized she gently picks his chin up and looks at him in the eyes, and says "Hello." Again smiling, at that the detective said shaking his stunning feeling he has and says pulling out his badge and said to her "My name is Detective James Smith." Smiling she asks "You are a man of authority?" Then the detective asks "What are you doing in the cemetery near this mausoleum, and who are you, where do you come from?" At that the eldest of the brothers Ondor approaches the detective and tells him "We need to talk away from this building alone, please follow me." Then he walks away from the mausoleum and turns to the detective and gestures him to follow him. So the detective follows him, intimidated a little bit by his sheer size, they walked a considerable distance, then Ondor begins to speak to the detective. Ondor tells the detective "By now you have probably have some information of what is inside this building, and it must not be good, as a matter of fact it is evil lurking inside that has gotten out." Looking at the detective Ondor asked him "Am I not right?" The detective hesitant to answer at first finally says "Somewhat." "Somewhat." Ondor repeats looking at him. "You still have not answered my questions." The detective said to Ondor. "Let me ask one more question and I will answer yours, fair enough?" Asked Ondor. Nodding the detective said "Yes" Looking at him then slightly tilting his head to one side he asked" has their lookout guardians attacked you or someone in this town, has anybody gotten hurt or killed?" "Guardians?" asked the detective. "Yes guardians, lookouts or attackers, they seek out their targets and will destroy them." Said another voice the detective turned around and it was the dark dressed woman Irina, who was looking at him with seriousness. Then she said to him "Can you walk with us to our vehicles?" They started to walk to their vehicles as they approached Jason could not believe his eyes the detective was walking with two tall persons he's never seen before, a woman as tall as he is and a man taller than he is. They walked to the black SUV and Ondor opened the door and took out a thick old book and opened it and turned pages and finally stopped and showed the detective the guardians they are speaking to him about as he looked he stayed looking at the pictures. Upon looking at the pictures he turned and looked at both Irina and Ondor at that Irina said "You have, haven't you, I can see you have, have you been injured?" At that the detective said "Now, answer my question, who are you? What are you doing here, where are you from?" At that Lord DarkWar approached the detective and the detective stayed looking at him, and then Lord DarkWar extended his hand out to shake his hand and proceeded to answer his questions. The detective stays looking at Lord DarkWar who towers over his sons a foot taller, he is eight foot tall has an appearance of a powerhouse body builder dressed in all black, eyes color black, Blackbeard, black hair to his shoulders, black tattoo marking on his arms, very intimidating. "So you want to know where we are from do you." He asked the detective. "I do." The detective said. "We are from central Europe we live in a private fortress with our family." "You've come a long ways just to look at this mausoleum?" The detective asked curiously. "Not just a mausoleum, a place of keeping of the condemned ones, with a seal to keep them in, which has been broken, now they have come out, and they have come out before." Lord DarkWar said. Silence has stricken the detective, all this he knows from all the investigating work he's done, and from talking to the living ancestors from the ones involved with the case from more than a hundred years ago, and those that has first contact with this thing. Not only that, but by talking to this Lord DarkWar, he's beginning to shed light on the whole thing. The detective asked "When you said seals did you mean those metal trims in front of the entrance of the door located on the top and on both sides?" "Those are the ones, undisturbed, they are powerful, and can hold evil in for all time, removed, and tinkered with, otherwise interfered with and they are limit in power, which happened in this case, it happened long ago and it happened recently." Lord DarkWar added. By hearing of the removal of the seal it started to make sense, those figures Jim was seeing was the condemned ones after him, Jim had sealed his own doom by removing the seal. Then Lord DarkWar said this in part answered your second question "What are we doing here?" "Yes, I do want to know just what exactly what you are doing here." The detective said. Lord DarkWar said "When learned the seals were broken and a person went missing and another one got hurt bad, we knew he had to go back and do something about it, these that are kept here are condemned for all time, they too are immortal like us but they practice sorcery evil and vile craft, this very town during its infancy had their trial and was found guilty of their crimes they were burned at the stakes, because they are immortals they can't die normally, we got their remains and locked them away, the burning altered their figures, they took on new forms, but remained evil nonetheless." "Do you expect me to believe that?" The detective asked with a doubtful look. "Do you require more proof?" Lord DarkWar asked. Then the detective said "More than that, I'm afraid," then Lord DarkWar said "Take me to your town hall of court records, there you will find exactly what you have been looking for." So the detective agreed, as they walked to the vehicles the detective saw Jason and remembered about him, and was about to tell him about going to the hall of and was going to give him a choice of either coming with him or going back to his apartment. At that Lord DarkWar asked the detective "Your companion is he coming with us, or going elsewhere?" Then the detective said "I'm going to take him back to his place." "Allow me to arrange that." Lord DarkWar said. He called his two daughters Amara and Irina and he said to them "Please take this young man back to his place of residence and take Jeff to his place of residence also, he's been most helpful." They both nodded and said "Yes father." Before the detective left with Lord DarkWar he told Jason "I'll return soon, Jason to check on you, ok?" "Sure." Said Jason as Jason got out of the car he looked and both daughters approached him and asked him "What is your name" Looking at both of them and speechless and awestricken two beautiful women very tall about six foot four both elegant looking, athletic looking, one in dark clothing the other light clothing, both wearing dresses, more like battle attire. Still looking at them he heard one of them say "We always have this problem with these males they seem as if they have not seen women like us at all." Then Jason finally came to and said "I have indeed, seen women, but not like you though, you're . . . ." "Tall" Said Irina, looking down at him. "And so beautiful." Jason said. They both smiled and looked at each other and then at him. Then they said "Thank you." "My name is Jason." He said. Then they both introduced themselves to him "Irina" the one in dark clothing said, "Amara" the one in light clothing said. Irina said to Jason "Now let's take you home, the detective will be by your home soon to check on you." Jason nodded they all got in one of the SUV's and drove off to first Jeff's place of residency then Jason's place of residence, they dropped off Jeff, and told him once more the helpfulness he has been to them then they drove off. As they drove to Jason's place, Amara asked Jason, "Why is the detective checking on you? Are you in trouble with the authorities?" Jason smiled and said "No, I was attacked three times." Both Amara and Irina said at the same time "Three times." And then they looked at each other and then Irina asked him "By whom?" Then Jason answered "Or what, something hit me hard at the cemetery I had to spent almost a year at the hospital." Then Irina asked him "What were you doing at the cemetery, when you got assaulted?" Then Jason answered "I was reading tombstones, don't ask why I like doing that, but I do, and upon reading them I wondered back at the cemetery where I saw something I was looking at that black marbled mausoleum." By that time this got both their attention and continued to listen to him. "Please continue." Said Amara they were still driving while Jason is telling them of his encounters. Then Jason continues "As I was walking I noticed that mausoleum front door was a little bit open about a few inches, I stood there looking into it trying to look inside the darkness then all so sudden real fast all I could see is a skull face coming at me sand hit he with great force, I flew back several feet and hit a couple of tombstones almost knocking them over." At that Irina pulled over and asked Jason "Go on." Then Jason continues "I must have blacked out or not remembered getting out of there, I remember waking up and talking to the detective, who was already working on another case, on the other guy that disappeared." Then Irina asked Jason "Did you know this other guy who disappeared?" "I have seen a couple of times but I do not know him personally." Jason said. Then Amara asked Jason "Is this all that has happened to you?" "No" Jason said "What else happened to you?" Amara asked. Then Jason said" Not long after I recovered from my injuries, something has been following me, try to get me, had it not been for the interference of other people I would have been doomed." "What has been following you" Irina asked. "You wouldn't believe me if I told you." "Try us" Irina and Amara both said at the same time. Jason said "Ok here it goes, not long after my recovery, a real big black bird about as tall as I am and a very big black dog both had evil glowing red eyes was and still after me, they unsuccessfully tried to get me, had it not been for some helpful people and a driver of a truck who tried hit that dog, I would of not been here talking to you." At that they both looked at each other and turned the SUV around and headed back to the cemetery. "Uh um where are we going, I'm supposed to go back home." Jason said. "Not anymore." Irina said "You are coming with us you are the one we are looking for." She added. Confused Jason asked Irina "How am I the one you are looking for?" Amara turned to him and told him "Your life is danger, you are being hunted, those things will not stop, until they finish what they set out to do, like this unfortunate Jim, you also, are destined to meet your fate, that's why those things are after you." At that Jason sunk to his seat and slouched. And said with much despair" But I did not take anything from that god forsaken place, why me?" At that Amara turned to comfort him and gently lifted his chin to look at him in the his eyes and say to him "Jason, you have seen something that was not meant to be seen by mortal humans, but have no fear, I have been sent here to protect you, I am your protector, I am to protect you from harm's way." "You will not be alone Jason, we can assure you of that, where ever you go Amara will be close." Irina said to Jason. Almost convinced with comfort Jason said "Ok." Jason asked Irina "Are you a protector also?" Then Irina said to Jason "Not quite, I'm a warrior, my sister is a protector." They headed to regroup with the other who has already left the cemetery and has gone back to their place of temporary place of residency. Meanwhile the detective and Lord DarkWar arrived at the court hall of records, to inquire the earliest records of the courts taken place in the town's history. As they walk inside the courthouse everybody stopped what they were doing and looked at the detective and his guest walking with him who is Lord DarkWar. All the people inside the building pulled out their cameras and started taking pictures of DarkWar and marveled at his size. As they were walking to the back room to the record room Lord DarkWar asked the detective "Is it just me or these people haven't seen a person like me before." Letting out a little chuckle the detective said "They are not use to seeing a person of sheer size." As they continued to walk to the records room he also said to Lord DarkWar, I have been coming here for years, for cases and such I'm a tall man by comparison to them, but walking next to you, I look short, that's why they are looking and taking photos and probably video clips of you walking with me." Nodding with acknowledgement Lord DarkWar continues walking with the detective. They arrive to the room they were looking for, they headed to the oldest part of the records, looking through the records the earliest they could find was the court records after the establishment of this country. After considerable searching the detective said to Lord DarkWar "Well it looks as if your so call proof doesn't exists." At that Lord DarkWar stayed looking at the shelves of boxes of books and was recalling the place where they would be kept before this country was established. Then he turned to the detective and asked him "Where's the archives, the matter of records?" at that they both walked around and looked and in a short time they found it, they found the real old part Lord DarkWar was looking for. There the trial and other early trials were recorded there and held, Lord DarkWar let the detective read for himself the whole pages involving the accused the jailers the executers jury judges, the whole thing. As he finished he looked at Lord DarkWar and asked him "How old are you?" Then he answered "I stopped counting after forty six hundred years." Looking down at the floor the detective started to say "Under normal circumstances I'd say you're crazy, but considering the latest events that's has happened I'm willing to go on a little faith." Then lord dark war looked at him strait in his eyes and told him" Then it should not surprise you, I know a warrior when I see one, you are or was a warrior not long ago, a warrior of your time, am I not right?" Looking at him a little surprised he asked him "How do you know I was a warrior?" Smiling at him he says to the detective "My friend, from one warrior to another, there is something inside of a man made born when he becomes a warrior and it never leaves him, other warriors can pick it up, I sensed it as soon as I seen you for the first time." Smiling the detective said "You are right, I was a what you call a modern day warrior I was a United States Special forces, I served for over twenty years, and I am retired, I have been for over fifteen years." "But you still have the discipline with you, living with it, abiding by It." asked Lord DarkWar. Smiling and nodding the detective said "Yes." Then Lord Dark War pulled out another folder connected to the original folder and showed the detective how the condemned ones use to look like before they were burned to the stake and changed their appearances. They sat down at a table and Lord DarkWar Began to go over the whole entire archive with the detective, from the activities that the condemned ones were doing to their apprehension, to their trials, to their sentence, to their execution carried out. After several hours the detective had a broad view of the whole thing, and he turned and looked and said to Lord DarkWar" They have been out before, I was doing investigating on a case involving a man that had disappeared Jim, upon doing the investigating, it was found out that those condemned things had been out before, more than a hundred years ago, I came across a case similar to mine that was more than a hundred years old, I looked through the case and the same thing, the tall heavy walking skeleton taking somebody back to where they came from into darkness to the black mausoleum." Nodding at him Lord DarkWar said "Someone tampered with the seal back then as they did not too long ago." The detective said to DarkWar" I have notice every time the seal is tampered with they come out, I have not heard them coming out on their own." "You're absolutely correct, but what is to stop them from coming out on their own, they have defeated the seals, and they know it, it will be a matter of time before they run amuck through your city or town detective, and a lot of people will be hurt or worse disappear or die." Lord DarkWar said. "What are you planning on doing, to these condemned ones?" The detective asked. At that Lord DarkWar asked the detective "Where is your police headquarters?" "It's down town about a half of mile from here." The detective said. "Take me there, there we put the weapons to destroy the condemned ones, my son Lonor tried fabricating an equivalent but was unsuccessful, he's actually a very good weapon maker and arson specialist." Lord DarkWar said. They put the books back, and put all as it was found and to the police station they went. As they were on the way to the station, the detective couldn't help but to ask" how do you know of your weapons stored at the station, I don't even know that." Then Lord DarkWar answered" Before the police station there was the arson building, a place to keep all the fire arms, in case the foreigners were to attack, all men of age would grab guns and weapons and would defend the town, there is a cellar under your places of confinements of prisoners." The detective looks at him with ever amazement, and tells him "You keep surprising me, you know more about this town's ancient history than anybody I know." They arrive at the police station and go to the holding cells and Lord DarkWar stays looking at the holding cells and says "These are not the ones, where are the others?" then the detective says "These are the ones sense I've been here." Then Lord DarkWar walks to the hallway looking remembering the way the inside was at one time, then he remembers, he goes to the detectives office and looks at a thick shelving and begins to move it sideways, then all of a sudden it moves, the detective jaw about drops looking at what is in his office all this time. Then Lord DarkWar looks downstairs and asks for light. Detective asks one of the officers for his flashlight then both the detective and Lord DarkWar go downstairs to look at the weapons. As they reached the final steps to the floor they looked around, and in an old heavy metal chest Lord DarkWar said "There, they are, the weapons we need to destroy the evil in the mausoleum, the condemned ones." The detective tried to move the chest, it is too heavy for him, and then Lord DarkWar says to him "Allow me detective." At that the detective moved aside and with one hand Lord DarkWar moved the chest out to the open. The detective stayed looking at him, his time with much intimidation. He thought to himself "This big guy can crush me with his bare hands at any moment, but thankfully he's the good guy . . . . I hope." Then looking at the detective he pulled out his necklace and pulled out an old key and opened the chest. Then they put the light in the chest looking inside at the contents, to the detectives amazements they are swords and shields and forearm bracelets, shin guards, and what seems to be knuckle guards to cover the whole fist. But these were not ordinary swords or shields, the detective can see this. They are made of special alloy metal, all this time kept in this environment and they do not rust. Then the detective said" this is that you are going to use on them?" Nodding at him Lord DarkWar said Yes, this is the only thing that can." Then he said to the detective, "All this other stuff is yours." The detective looked around with his flashlight and could see all kinds of rifles pistols, kegs of powder, cannons, he was indeed surprised. At that he said to Lord DarkWar "You never stop surprising me." Lord DarkWar said to the detective "We need to get this chest to my vehicle as soon as possible," They closed and locked the chest and called four officers to help carry the chest out of the cellar and on to the vehicle of DarkWar, he didn't want lord DarkWar to freak everybody out with his strength, then both he and the detective drove off to meet the rest of the group. They arrive at their place of lodging, Ryoc managed to rent them a sizable house, instead of a hotel, now everyone had a room, and in comfort, and privacy, they moved Jason in with them for the time being, to keep him from harm's way, there is no way he'll be safe in his apartments by himself. The detective and Lord DarkWar stopped by the cemetery to get his car and then follow the SUV to the house they rented. Upon arriving, he sees Jason with Amara and Irina, and waves at him to come to him, Jason comes to him and sees what he has to say. "Jason, are you staying with these people?" The detective asked. "They learned I am the one that's in danger of those things, and they refuse to leave me by myself." Nodding the detective said to Jason "Don't give them any static, ok?" Jason then nodded. Lord DarkWar parked the SUV and called out his sons, to take down the chest and bring it in the house. After bringing the chest in the house Ondor the eldest of the son approached the detective and showed him small samples of the alloy he managed to manufacture, but it want enough to make any kind of weapon that will inflict harm to the condemned ones such as a knife or dagger or sword. There is a hundred pieces of the alloy, he showed the detective, then detective stayed looking at them, then he asked "How much trouble is it to make them into a cylinder shape with a point, the size they are?" looking at them he said "Probably none, it will several hours, depending how hot we get the fire going." Ondor said. Looking at the detective Ondor can see the detective has an idea to use the pieces of metal, and asks the detective "You have an idea for these?" Then the detective said to Ondor, "I use to be in special forces in the military I was a weapons specialists, if I can shape theses into cylinder shape with a point, it will create a very harmful weapon for the condemned ones." "My father is right, you are a warrior." Ondor said. So they went to work on the pieces of metals to form them into cylinders to fit a fifty caliber gun. The detective knew a metal shop with the latest state of the art metal fabricating equipment they can rent. They rented the shop and fabricated the rounds to fit a fifty caliber gun. When all is done they had a total of one hundred rounds, which meant they have to be careful not to be wasteful with the bullets. Being of military the detective went to his house and pulled out his secrete stash of guns, specifically the fifty caliber automatic gun with a silencer. The gun has its own stand, and its case of accessories. They went to show what they did with the pieces of the special alloy Ondor made to Lord DarkWar. By the time they arrived at their house it was nightfall, Jason was getting ready for bed, his room is right across from Irina's and next to Amara's Jason falls asleep and Irina and Amara watch him for a little while, making sure he'll be fine, then satisfied all is well, they go their room and settle in for the night. Meanwhile elsewhere in the house the detective and Ondor shows Lord DarkWar the good use the pieces of the special alloy are put, into special rounds fitted for a fifty caliber gun, and he's impressed. Then the detective said he's going to call it the night, and he'll see them sometime tomorrow, and he left back to his home. During the night Jason begins to have nightmares of the big dog and bird attacking him and trying to taking him to the cemetery to the mausoleum, he starts to breath faster and panting in his sleep, this wakes up Amara and Irina, and they quickly go in and check on Jason by then he's tossing and turning and moaning and staring to yell, Irina places her hand on his leg to try to calm him down and he jumps out of bed and doesn't knows where he is and Amara catches him and holds him and calms him down. Jason wakes only to find himself in Amara's arms like a child and is embarrass and turns all kinds of shades of red and, looks at her and Irina and puts his head down goes to bed without saying anything. Covers his whole body so they wouldn't see him, and he wouldn't see them. "You want to talk about it, Jason?" asked Amara. "No." Jason said in an embarrassing undertone. They were about to leave the room and Jason uncovered himself and said "I need to go home." Amara said to Jason "You know you can't go to your apartment, it's too dangerous." Jason continued "to my parents' home, where I use to live, before I left or got kicked out to get my medicine." Looking at Jason Irina asked "Why did you leave or got kicked out as you put it?" Jason got up and looked at her and said "Favoritism, my little sister is spoiled and is favored by all, by my parents and little brother, my father even told me I'll never amount to anything, I hate him, but I need my meds." Looking at each other Irina and Amara said "Well take you there tomorrow, to get your meds, ok?" Jim nodded. Then Jason said "I had a nightmare, that big dog was after me and so was that big bird, and it felt real, maybe because I was attacked already. "Then he lifted his shirt and showed them his scars and marks left by the dog and bird. Both Amara and Irina stayed looking at them and him. Then they asked him "Does your parents know of this?" "They could care less all they care is about my little sister, favoritism." Jason said. Amara sat on the bed beside him and asked him "Jason, how old are you?" looking at her he said "twenty seven." Then she said "You're old enough to be alone if that's what you desire." Finally the nightmare sufficed, and all went to bed morning came and Jason woke and couldn't move freely to aside, he felt as if he was being held, he turned and sure enough it was Amara who had slept with him looking over him on his bed, not truly convinced of his nightmare being over. Jason secretly admittedly to himself it felt good to be held by a woman a rather tall beautiful woman. He got up as quietly as he could and as little movement as not to disturb Amara them he was going then he bumped into Irina who was looking at him. Then she said "Good morning Jason, I see had a good night's sleep." Jason stayed looking at her and before he could say anything he heard Amara behind him say "Jason, you are up, ok, let's all freshen up and go downstairs and start our morning." At that all went to do so. As Jason had his morning meals with this family he saw they are not different in appearance and functions than he is except they are bigger stronger, and immortal. After their morning meals their father Lord DarkWar led his sons and daughters to the extra room in the back to the chest they sons put back there yesterday, they opened the chest and all looked in and knew which their weapon to take is. Then they went to the back yard to brush up on their special powers they all each had, Jason was in for a surprise to see them use them. Lord DarkWar had prepared some targets to use with their powers to practice, it's been a while since they have battled the forces of evil, now they will have to do so once more minus one, and Amara has to stay behind to protect Jason from the eminent danger coming his way, which is sure to take him to his doom. Irina could stay to help her sister protect Jason, but given the nature of the situation, the evil woman in the mausoleum might try her trickery on her elder brother Ondor once more, long ago they use to be lovers, until her dark secrets were discovered, and as a result she and her dark ones were charged, tried found guilty and executed. Now they found a way to defeat the seals and now may try to kill him or have him killed, which she will not allow nor his brothers or father, but she feels it's a female thing, and she can sense her trying her dark powers over brother and that's when she'll intervene. As Jason sat on the back steps he watched with utter shock as one by one they annihilated their targets with their powers. Not only are they all physically strong and powerful, their powers are unbelievable. First, the eldest son Ondor steps up he's wearing his battle attire which is black in color armor is that color of pewter sleeveless jacket/coat with partial armor, pants to match, if you want to call them pants, and boots that looks as if they match, which they look, armor plated. He steps up at his target and all of a sudden his tattoo markings stat to move and glow and so does his hair and eyes as if a blur surrounded him and a hum can be heard surrounding him then he hits his target made of a cemented pile of stone, very solid. Then with two hits one on top one on bottom, his target was no more. All was left is a pile of rubble. The next son steps up who precedes his elder brother Ionor the one in yellow who is dressed like his brother but in yellow, not yellow but shadow yellow very discrete, he too has tattoo markings like his brother and when he activated his powers they also started to move and glow his color yellow as his hair and eyes and a hum. He threw a punch and then a round house kick at his target made of a slab of concrete, and it crumbled. Jason stayed looking at their awesome display of power. After Ionor his brother after him stepped up, Kion the one in blue like his brothers, he too has powers he is dressed in color blue is a shadow blue, like his brothers so are his eyes hair and tattoo markings, he too activated his powers and the markings started to move and glow as his hair and eyes and a hum the target is a standing cemented together logs, he threw two punches and the logs splintered apart with flying cement debris. Next is his brother that proceeded him Ryoc, the one in green, is armor is that like his brothers but shadow green like his brothers his tattoo markings move when his powers activate the markings move and glow green as does his hair and eyes and hits his target before him a boulder taller than he is two punches and the boulder breaks into a few pieces. His brother after him the youngest one Endor who is the red one, he like his brothers has armor but is shadow red, like his brothers he has tattoo markings that glow and move when he activates his powers as his hair and eyes, he activates his powers and before him is a block of cemented together layered concrete blocks, he punches the blocks twice and the block is busted up and crumbled. Next is the daughters, the first one Irina dressed in her battle attire in a fighting dress skirt, with partial armor in black, her boots has a shin armor. She like her brothers has markings but not as visible as her brothers but famine lighter color she too can activate her powers and her markings start to move and glow as her eyes and hair but not as her brothers, but in a very elegant powerful way and a slight hum. She walks up to her target which is a an old stone filled dumpster she throws a punch and knocks a hole in it and does a roundhouse kick and hits the dumpster and it flies several yards into the back wooded area out of sight. Next is her younger sister Amara dressed like her sister but only in lighter almost white, off-white she too like her sister has markings very light but more visible when her powers activate she walks up to her target which is a wall of logs tied together and layer of bricks in between all tied together, she punches right through it log bricks and does a round house kick and totally destroys the wall. Finally the father, Lord DarkWar he is in his battle attire which appears to be older than his sons and daughters, and a little different he also has sleeveless and the marking are much greater than his sons. Before him are a few targets, a large marble slab that looks like a monument, a large concrete block that looks like a counterweight of a Crain, and a tall pillar made of granite. He activates his powers and his markings move and glows and so do his eyes and hair and a slightly louder hum. He threw one punch to the marble stone it goes flying in two pieces with other pieces in between crumbling, then he punches the concrete block it breaks in half but the re-enforced bars held it from crumbling, then he round house kicked the pillar made of granite it broke in the middle with a crumble. As they finished their practicing, the detective who had arrived for some time had seen the whole thing. And was speechless, for he still could not believe what he just witnessed. He made his way to the front of the house as to not give the impression he was ease dropping on them. He rings the doorbell then he knocks, and he waits, then the door opens and Kion answers the call, lets him in and leads him to the den where the rest of the group is. Jason tells Amara he needs to go to his parents' home and get his medicine, so Irina and Amara take Jason to get his medicine from his parents' home. They leave on their SUV to Jason's parents' house, on the way Amara asked Jason, "If you don't mind me asking, why you need that medicine at your parents' house, can you not get another one, since you seem not to get along with them?" "The medicine if for when I had bad nightmares, I haven't had them in a long while, until this happened to me, I figured it would help me, now that I know I can have nightmares now." Jason said. As they approached his parents' home, Jason started getting more nervous, and tense, Amara and Irina can already see that. "Are you going to be alright?" asked Amara. "I'm just going in to get it and go out." Jason said. They stopped Jason sat still for a while and looked at the house, his eyes got tearful and he got down and walked to the front door and knocked on the front door, and he waited. What Jason did not expect is any kind of support from Amara and Irina, which is going to happen. Without Jason realizing it, Amara and Irina already had gotten off the SUV and made their way near the front door, the front yards trees made it possible for them to hide. The front door opened it is his little brother, Scott, "Hey Jason, what are you doing here?" he asked. Jason said "I have come for my medicine that's in my room." Before anything could be said his father shows up and looks at him with utter disgust and says to him "What the hell do you want, I told you, there's nothing here for you." "I need the medicine in my room." Jason said. "That became a guest room, it's no longer your room, and all your stuff is gone." His father told him. "Well do you know where is at, I really do need it." Jason said. "I'll ask your mother, stay out here, I'll be back." When he left to talk to Jason's mother, Jason looked depressed, and his younger brother was trying to talk to him until his father said loudly "Scott get over her now." As Scott left the door Amara and Irina gently stepped up the front porch where Jason is and was standing behind him, they heard his father say to his brother "You don't want to be like your brother, a damn homo, and a loser." A short while passed by and his mother showed up at the front door and said "We threw everything out, I'm sorry we didn't think you needed it." "Don't apologize to him he's nobody to apologize to." His father said from inside the house. Before Jason could say anything Amara and Irina stepped into view and defended Jason from his parent's remarks. Irina stood in front of the door, Jason's mother looked up at her and Irina told her in a bold tone "Woman! You are a poor excuse for a mother a real mother would not discard what may be in need for her child." Looking up at Irina, she asks "Who are you, and what are you doing with my son." "Who we are is none of your business, and what we are doing with your son is his business, and why are you so concerned now for him, he's in better company than he was with you." Irina said to her "He's my son I have the right to know." His mother said to Irina "That's a real laugh coming from you, from what I just heard you just tell him, you discarded his medicine, you didn't think he didn't need it." Irina told her. "Is he arguing with you? I'll be right over there." His father shouted. "I told you there is nothing here for you, so quit bothering your mother or I'll stomp a mud hole in your ass." He said was he waked to the front door. As he walked to the front door he opened the front door expecting to find his son Jason, instead he found his wife still looking at up two tall women looking at her, and now him with Jason looking down at the floor. "Who are you?" he asked. "Who we are is not important, you must be that poor excuse for a father of his." Irina said to him. "Come again." He said to Irina. "You are pathetic, your son is not a loser, nor is he gay." Amara told him. "Just who are you to come to my house and tell me such things." He snapped back. "Because you so full of yourself you see no other things but your own narrow views." Irina told him. "And perhaps it is you that needs to have a mud hole stomped in you dry." She added. "Oh really! I'd like to see you try it. "He re-butted back. At that both Irina and Amara picked him out of his house and lifted up and were about to punch him to the other side of the yard but Jason said "Stop, leave him, let's go." Jason started to walk off and Amara and Irina dropped him, and he fell to the floor and walked after him and Irina said "let's go, he doesn't deserve a son like you, at all, what he really needs to do is check on his perfect daughter who gets too much privacy, when her friends come over and he seems to worship her so much." They walked off to their SUV to drive off, Amara turned around and picked him up from the floor and stand him up and told him "We are not vile, were good people, we just can't stand people with your frame of mind, very narrow view, your son, is a very fine young man, what's wrong is you, and your lack of virtue. Your son had been injured and hospitalized for almost a year, after an attack from unspeakable evil even though he's in danger of getting killed from what we're protecting him from he still tries to go by himself as if nothing, that's brave." She walked off and got on the SUV and they drove off. As they drove off Jason was very quiet, had nothing to say. Amara said to Jason "I'm sorry for what you just went through, some people can't be helped, and they are who they are." Then Jason said "If I would have let you beat my father, it would only add weight to his accusations, and knowing my mother she would have called the police, and it would have been a mess." He turned to Amara and asked her" Why did you tell my father to check on my sister, the perfect one." She turned to him and said "Jason, when you had told me about your position with your family and all the favoritism going on, it was quite obvious what is going on, your sister is up to no good, your parents ignoring it, busy on you giving you a hard time." Jason had a not so sure look on him. They continued to drive off. After they drove off Jason's father stood outside for almost an hour trying to come in terms to what just happened, he could of gotten hurt real bad almost an hour ago, but his son stopped it, had his son been like himself he would of let the assault take place with his frame of mind you need this to become a better person reasoning. But he didn't. As he continued thinking he realized, his son is not gay, because he is with two big and tall beautiful women, granted he was about to get stomped, they are women nonetheless. And his son is not a loser, for someone who knows nothing about their family history of troubles, of accusations they see contrary, and someone totally different with bravery. He finally went inside his house, "Are you alright dear, shall I call the police?" his wife asked him. Shaking his head he said "No, maybe I was a little to rude and a little too extreme for him and inconsiderable, even in front of two complete stranger." They decided to check on their daughter who has not opened her door since after school, it's now close to dinner time, both he and his wife opened the door and much to the tall woman's comments about their daughter's perfection, she was caught in the act having an intimate relationship with another girl her age. Both he and his wife closed the door with their mouths wide open and went to the kitchen table. The father whose name is Michael is looking at the table telling his wife, Linda "What have I've done, my son hates me no doubt, and with good reason." Linda asked him "What is his life in danger of, what injured him?" "I doubt if Jason ever wants to speak with us ever after today." Michael said. Then Michael said to Linda "Go, send our daughters friend home right now, we have to talk to our daughter, tell Scott to visit his friend for at least two hours." Linda nodded, and then she took her friend home and both Michael and Linda had a very serious talking to their daughter Rachel. After the talking Rachel was reprimanded and was prohibited from having any friends come over or phone calls from any of her friends. Furthermore because of her age, it is thought it would be best for her to be removed from school environment and be put into home schooling. Usually Michael would be very harsh towards this kind of behavior towards his children, but due to these events that just unfolded, it is making him a different man. While there on their way back, Amara asked Jason if we would be ok without his medicine, Jason had responded with a not so sure answer which caused some concern for her, so she saw it would be a good idea for both her and her sister to keep looking after Jason and calm him if he has any more nightmares. As they arrived from their way back from Jason's parent's home, the detective is still inside talking to their father and brothers. As they went inside the detective is listening to Lord Dark War's plans of drawing them out and attack, and finally putting an end to their evil, and no more humans will be neither killed nor consumed. As they walked in their father, Lord DarkWar turned to Jason and said to him "Jason please sit, we need to have a discussion that involves you." He also turned to his two daughters and told then also to sit, they all including the detective at the dining room table. Lord DarkWar begins to outline the battle due to take place with the condemned ones, from drawing them out, to ambushing them to annihilate them one and for all. Then all eyes in the dining room turn to Jason as lord DarkWar asks Jason for a small favor. "Jason, I have a small favor to ask of you." Looking concern, but willing to help he asks, "Sure, what's your favor you ask?" Then Lord DarkWar continues "We need a bait to draw them out, if one of us did it, they would know, and will not come out, or try to ambush us one by one, that's why I would like to ask you to remove the seal so they can sense it and come after you." Looking all so gloomy thinks of his messed up family life and reasons within himself why not, I'll never will amount to anything anyways in the eyes of my father. Jason asks "You want me to seal my doom like Jim did, why not, I have nothing to lose?" Amara firmly told Jason "Were going to protect you, unlike this Jim, who remove the seal on his own, you are backed up and will not be allowed to be harmed Jason." "My daughter is right Jason, you will be protected against this evil, and you are speaking as if your life is worthless, no life is worthless, one's life may be full of disappointments but are precious nonetheless." "All my children, are cunning warriors, Amara, may be the youngest of my children but she is powerful, cunning, and will protect you, if things get too hectic, Irina will back her up, Jason you have nothing to fear." Lord DarkWar said. Nodding Jason stayed quiet for the duration of the discussion. The detective said "No weapons of ours can hurt them, vehicles can just bump them out of the way or deter them, but they'll be back, I know your weapons can kill them, destroy them, I realize you couldn't replicate the metal in time, just small quantities, so with some help I am able to make some projectiles made from this metal to combat them." The detective also added "These will have the same effect on them as your weapons do except they can't see these coming they travel in a high rate of speed, and will punch right through them." Ondor asked "What about the people who may be around, and may be caught in this mess?" Then the detective said "That's why we're going to have a curfew for a few nights and since the cemetery is located on the edge of town, well make roadblocks." The detective also added "Very few individuals know about this, the police force and some pedestrians who has seen some of these things in action and were made to keep quiet for safety sake." One of the most important information is about to be discussed with the detective from the family of warriors, it is the origin of the condemned ones and their evil tactics and powers they used on their victims, their transformations from their original form, and possible power changes. Lord DarkWar starts with the biggest of the condemned ones the walking skeleton with a black trench coat and log black hat, Lord DarkWar stars with him and says "This one is the muscle, of the condemned ones, the enforcer, the one who they sent to destroy, capturer the hunter, this one does not fail when it comes to getting his bounty. We call him Tall back, because of his tallness, and he does not slouch nor bend in manners that suggest he's lax. He's powerful and heavy and will require more than usual to put him down, once he's put down, immediately, destroy him. Do not delay, if he does get up, hurt he might be, he'll become more fierce and harder to put down, so don't delay once he is down, don't toy with him, and thinking you'll ware him down, it will only feed the rage and make him stronger. Avoid his swings to hit, they are nothing but power, and can injure or kill in most cases (if your mortal), although he's never been seen throwing kicks, he is capable, and are just as deadly if you are fighting him, and manage to break off a limb of his, be cautious, he's just as deadly without it, he's so tall he looks as if he only walks, don't be fooled, he strides he takes are so long he has no need for running or moving fast, and yes he can get to places pretty quick. His strength is of unearthly power, he can bust through rock, stone cement walls, thick log, and cement walls." After he finished a small time of silence filled the room. The next one Lord DarkWar starts to talk about is the hooded one, the one that resembles death, but without the sickle. Lord DarkWar starts to say" This one is the bringer of bad news, the warning of coming dire consequences, the bringer of darkness we call him hooded one. He walks around in his hood to conceal his altered self, no one has seen his without his hood we know how he looked before his burning of the stake, now his altered for is all but a mystery, but he is not to be underestimated, he has stealth speed strength and deadly accuracy, and can see in places other cant. He can make himself be unseen for periods of time for mortals, which explain why this Jim only saw him partially, but enough to paralyze him with fear. He is as tall as "tall back" is, he does talk but in a very subtle kind of way, enough to get your attention, and enough for his victims to understand, they are doomed." When he finished talking again everyone was quiet. They reached the last of the condemned ones, the lady that that looks long dead, and the mischeaviouse one. Lord DarkWar starts to speak but pauses and looks at his eldest son, and says to him "Ondor my son, with your permission I would like to tell of this one and her backgrounds with you and havoc caused and caused to so many other ones." Nodding in agreement Ondor says to his father "That's quite alright father, she is a devil and needs to be destroyed, and I no longer have any feelings or ties with her." With a respectable nod, Lord DarkWar starts to speak "This one, the woman who looks long since dead we call her woman of death, because that is what she brings to all her victims, she lures them tricks them, then she brings them death. She tried to lure my son, but my son is wise beyond his years and recognized her trickery and cunning ways, and had her own evil work against her." As his father was answering questions about the woman, from both Jason and the detective, Ondor drifted back into a distant past, remembering when he and the condemned woman who was known back then as Victoria were lovers courting, little did he know she was already trapping and luring would be victims into their death, a very beautiful and deadly cunning woman she was, for some odd reason she did nothing to Ondor, she was helplessly in love with him, every time she was around him his very presents was intoxicating for her, she was paralyzed with love. When they were together, she marveled at him, and his masculine body and looks, it was almost as if she was blinded with love. Everything was so picture perfect until his sister Irina started to notice something dark about her, something did not seem right nor did it feel right. Death was in her company everywhere she went, death followed, every man who fell for her beauty and dark spells ended up dead. Irina did not want her brother to fall under her dark spell she began to follow and note all her dealings with town's locals and follow disappearances, of rival lovers such as other woman, who loves the same man she intended to lure and murder. The news Irina had to tell her brother was very heartbroken and despairs, but he needed to know the truth. At first Ondor was in denial and angry at his sister, but when the truth was revealed and he himself witnessed the once love of his commit this terrible act of murder, he had no choice to condemned her, it pained him at first, to do so, but after what Irina showed him beyond a doubt, and assured him it was out of love for her brother that she did what she did. When they were tried and is to be executed she kept telling him of her love and how she couldn't bring herself to harm him and his very presents is very intoxicating to her, he was the reason why she was changing. But it was too late, all the blood spilled on her account was too much to dismiss. His thinking of the past was broken when his sister Irina asked him "Are you ok?" then he said "Yes of course." By that time, Lord DarkWar had finished with the questions Jason and the detective had asked. Then their discussion came for the last two of the condemned ones the big bird black bird and the big black dog. Lord DarkWar said "Our first up is the big bird this big bird is black, black as the darkest night with eyes of evil glowing red this bird is almost as tall as a midsize man (looking at Jason) it will attack and it will tear and rip its intended target the detective looked at him and them looked at his shirt covering chest then looked back at Lord DarkWar. Then DarkWar continues "It will track and follow any one, anything of interest and through its eyes the condemned ones and see a wide broad view of points of interest. Its horrific screams is intended to ward off all intruders in a sacred area, if ignored it will follow and wreak havoc to the ones it follows, finally attacks, its flying cannot be heard, its stealthy, and its victims will not notice till it's too late. It's capable of picking up objects heavier than its self then flying off to their doom. Because of its mutated state, he's nearly impossible to bring down, watch for his swooping from above if he don't grab you hell gouge you, if he decides he can land and grapple with you, blinding with his wide wing span and clawing and scratching you and don't forget his bill or beak just like a hook tears and rip at anything, finally do not let this big bird pin you to the ground he will tear you up piece by piece." He ended saying looking at the detective and Jason. Then Lord DarkWar reaches the last one of discussion the big black dog. "Our last but not least is the mutated mutt from hell, this big black dog, is darker than black its self and its eyes is pure evil if you look into its eyes too long it will consume you. Its size is that of small pony but heavier and is beyond normal beyond control of mortal ones. This one has been known to maul its victims to death, leaving them unrecognizable, nothing but ground up flesh and bone. His running speed is that of a horse, is victims cannot run from him, he can also pounce from a distance and he can also jump high to snatch his victims in high places they thought was unreachable. Hiding in a place he can't fit might but you time but he will wait it out. Sometimes he'll dig you out. You will have to, sooner or later come out, or die in your hiding. He is the scout of the condemned ones at night is the perfect time through his eyes, the condemned ones can see up close so keep your distance at all times, and if you do clime, perhaps a house or a small hill top or tree make sure it's a steep angle and tall where it can't jump and grab or pounce you, if he does either way your through." As they finished discussing all of the condemned ones and their dark abilities, Lord DarkWar now begins to outline the base of attack and the best time to attack and ambush them. After all is said Lord DarkWar turns to Jason and asks him" Jason, are you ready to help us put end to this reign of terror?" With much assurance he got from Lord DarkWar and Amara and Irina he said "Yes." With the look of approval Lord DarkWar nodded and said to all at the table" Remember, these will not come after him immediately they will scout him and follow him in different places, we have to make that work to our advantage, lure them in places where a battle can happen with minimum attention and damage to both pedestrians and property." Meanwhile back at Jason's family's house, his father is thinking of just what kind of danger his son is in and what he is doing with those Amazons that nearly gave him a beating of untold proportions. All this time since they left, he's been reevaluating his entire course of action and attitude he had towards his son. The more he thought of the past the worse he felt no more than ever wanting to make amends with his son and first born. As he sat outside the porch of his house the police stopped by every house in the neighborhood and were announcing a curfew to take place, under a guise of an escaped convict heading this way. They reached his house and got off and begin to say to him" Good day." He looked at then with concern and responded back to the officers "Good day to you too." Then the officers continued "The reason why we're here is we are issuing a curfew starting tonight." Looking again with more concern he asked them "Something wrong?" Then the officers told him "There is an escaped convict on the loose believed to be headed this way, he is a dangerous criminal on death row, and had killed, so for your safety and your family stay inside your house listen to the radio and it will keep you informed, by no means are you to wonder the streets." With utter despair he looks at them and says to them "I have a son out there." Then the officers asked him "What is your son's name?" "Jason." Then they said "Well look for him." The advantage of a not so big town is everyone knows just about everyone.

As soon as they left he decided to go to the police station to talk to an officer about his son and the situation with his family and the danger he was told he is in. "Linda, I'll be back, I'm going to the police station to see about the danger my son is in and report it to the police." Michael told his wife. He drove off to the police station, thinking on how he's going to come about this to the police, after thinking he arrives at the station, by that time the detective is already in his office working on cases and filing them away. We walked in and begin ask the officer in the front desk" Can you please help me my son might be in danger?" "Who is your son?" The officer asked. Then he said "Jason." Then the officer said ok, have a seat, and someone will be with you shortly." So he sat on the chairs in front of the officer's desk. It seemed like ten minutes passed by, and Detective John Smith came to the front lobby where Michael is seated and asked him to follow him to his office. As they sat down the detective asked him "I understand your son is in danger, do you know from what?" Then Michael says "I don't know exactly what he's in danger of, but he is in danger, he spent a year in the hospital recovering, now was attacked not too long ago." The detective gave him a hard look for a while, and then he asked "His name wouldn't happen to be Jason?" Surprisingly Michael looked at him and asked "How did you know?" The detective then told him "He never told me he had family, as a matter of fact he lives in an apartment by himself." Just to confirm Jason is the same Jason he is speaking to Michael about he asked fundamental questions. "How old is Jason?" the detective asked Michael. "Twenty seven." He answered. Then he asked "How tall is he?" "About my height." Then he asked "When is the last time you seem him?" Michael said "Late this morning." Then he asked him "Was he alone?" "No." Michael answered. Then he asked "Do you know with whom?" Then Michael paused for a moment and said "You're going to find this hard to believe." Then the detective said "Try me." Then Michael says" Ok, here it goes, I saw him last at my house, arguing and he was with two very tall women." Looking at him the detective repeated "Two very tall women." "I know it's hard to believe, but it's true." Michael said. The detective asked "How tall are they?" Unsure Michael said "About your height." Then Michael continued "Look detective, I know you think I'm messing around with you, but I'm not, those two women told me after an argument he was in danger, and left." then the detective got up and closed the door to his office with only Michael and himself, then he sat back down and said to him" Ok, let me clarify something for you, and you are not to divulge anything to anybody. Except your wife, are we clear on that Michael." Michael then nodded then the detective continues "Those two tall women you saw, those are his protectors, and yes he is in danger of getting killed, by an evil I have yet to understand, yes he was attacked and yes he spend almost a year in the hospital, with a lot of broken bones, and yes he was just recently attacked." With a dire concern Michael asked "Do you know what attacked my son?" Then the detective asked him "Do you remember about a year ago the disappearance of a town local name Jim?" Michael said "I heard some of it, he was chased by a huge skeleton, corps, a dead lady, a big black dog and a big bird, and his car was found still running with the door ripped out and report of screaming and crying could be heard in the cemetery going to the old part towards the old mausoleums, and was never heard from again something like that." Nodding the detective said "Ok, so you know what we're talking about, Jason was walking the cemetery and wondered back to the old part to where the mausoleums are, he saw the door opened which it shouldn't of been, and something came out and attacked him, threw him back with such force he flew about twenty feet or so hitting and knocking over a couple of old tombstones." Michael asked the detective "Is there any way I can speak to my son?" The detective shook his head and said "For your own safety, and your own good, stay at your home, until this thing is over, the curfew is just a cover, but still stay in, if those things see anybody they will attack." Michael just sunk in his chair and looked down at the floor. The detective assured him "Michael, he's in good hands, I know that family, and they will not allow him to get hurt." Michael looked up and asked "What family?" As soon as he asked what family Lord DarkWar and his sons and daughters walked in his office. Michael could not believe his eyes, he saw Lord DarkWar who stood eight foot tall, followed by his sons who stood seven foot tall, and then his two daughters both stood about over six foot. Lord DarkWar said to the detective "We're making final preparations for tonight." Then the detective said "Ok, good." Then he looked at Lord DarkWar and pointed at Michael and said "This is Jason's father."

Lord DarkWar turned to Michael and looked at him and gave him one long nod. Michael nodded back. Then his sons followed, then his two daughters gave him a frown, Lord DarkWar noticed this and cleared his throat looking at his two daughters, then they nodded at Michael, Jason's father. Michael nodded back and got up and said to the detective," I have to go." And he left in a hurry, with a wet spot in front of his pants beginning to show. The detective asked "Where is Jason?" Then Amara said "He's in the vehicle sleeping." Nodding the detective continued with the details with the final preparations. When the final preparations were completed, all in the department knew their part, and will enforce the curfew. Meanwhile Lord DarkWar and his family went driving back to their house to let Jason rest for tonight. On the way he was thinking about the little fiasco between the man sitting in the detective's room and his daughters, and as soon as they settled down he was going to get to the bottom of it. They arrived at their house and Lord DarkWar asked Irina and Amara to join him in the den. He went in first then they followed him, and he asked them to sit. And then he asked them in a curious concern manner I need to ask you "What happened at the station between you and that man sitting in the detective's room, you looked at him ugly and he got scared and left in a hurry, wetting his pants?" Then they said "Father we are honored by you and our family and what it stands for, the man you saw, the man we frowned at is Jason's father." "And why is that bad, why did you look at his though he did wrong?" Lord DarkWar asked. "When we took Jason to his parents' house, to get his medicine to help with his nightmares, his family had alienated him, his father, that man in the detective's office accused Jason of loving the same gender as he is, Jason is not that way, and he is also abusive with his talking, making Jason almost cry." Irina said to her father. Lord DarkWar looked in disbelief and said "Go on." Then Amara said "His mother of all people who should care about her offspring threw his medicine away because she didn't think he needed it, what kind of a mother is she." "Every mother is different, every child is different." Lord DarkWar said. "Yes father we know, but every mother has that instinct of caring for her young her child, this one doesn't." Irina said. Then Lord DarkWar remembered earlier during their discussion when he asked Jason if he would not mind being used as bait to set traps for the condemned ones, and Jason responded as if he had nothing to lose, and if his life is worthless, and he remembered telling Jason of life not being worthless, all life is precious, then it all made sense. Then he rounded up all his sons and asked his daughters where Jason's parent's place of residence is and all the males went there to talk to the family. Before they left, he told his daughters to keep Jason safe until they return. They all left in one SUV to Jason's parent's house to talk to his parents about Jason. Not long after they left Jason woke up and found himself in bed, last place he remembered he was in was inside the SUV sleeping now he woke up in bed and doesn't remember how he got there. As he got up he looked around, and saw nobody then he waked around, the house is a bit roomy and large and because he has not seen nobody he was getting nervous. Then he saw both Irina and Amara sitting in the den talking about what happened today in the detective's office. Jason walks in and they both stopped talking and looked at him and Amara said "Did you have a nice sleep?" Jason said "Kind of." Then he sat across them and asked them "How I got to bed, I don't remember getting off the vehicle and going inside, I'm just wondering?" Then Irina looks at Amara and then looks at Jason then says to him" Oh, it's because you were carried in, all that restlessness you had, from those nightmares took a toll on you, we couldn't wake you up so you were carried in." Then they both smiled at him. Jason put his head down with embarrassment then barely looked up and asked "Who carried me in?" then without saying anything Irina looked at Amara and Amara smiled at him, then Jason put his head completely down, he couldn't look at them no more. In his mind he was just embarrass, a mature man carried like a child inside their house by a woman. "Would you rather have my brothers or our fathers carry you inside to bed, Jason?" Irina asked. Looking up more confused Jason said "How about making sure I wake up and I go inside myself." He said with a low embarrass tone. They just smiled at Jason they knew he is embarrassed by him learning he was carried in like a little child. Meanwhile, Lord DarkWar and his sons just arrived at Jason's parent's house. It was past noon time close to early evening when Michael's household heard a knock, Scott answered the door it is Endor the one in red Scott could not believe his size, he is much taller than those two women he saw before, but little did Scott know they are related, they are his sisters, his father saw them in the same room, however, his attention was mostly on the two women frowning at him that had his attention, therefore it might be possible his father may not of recognize them. Opening looking at him Scott said "Yes can I help you sir?" Then Endor begins to say" Yes, is the man of the house here, your father?" Still looking at him, he says "Um, ah, just a minute." He then closes the door slightly then he goes and gets his father. A short time his father comes to the door, looks up and stays looking at Endor, who is much taller than his sisters, towering over them right around seven foot tall. Looking up at him not too sure what he wants or what he's here for Michael asks him "Can I help you?" Then Endor says "My father would like to speak with you, about your son Jason." At that moment he was a little surprised and nervous, and said to him "Last ones who came in the same black SUV to talk to me about my son picked me off the ground, and was about to hit me, so please forgive me if I do not want to go with you anywhere." Endor kindly said to Michael "Were not here to hit no one nor pick them up from the ground, or otherwise do physical harm, I can assure you." Michael stayed looking at him and then he looked past him to the black SUV the same one that came before with Jason and those two tall women, then he asked "Is that your vehicle?" Then Endor said "Yes, it is, why?" Then Michael said "It's a lot like the other one that was driven here before" then Endor said nodding "Oh yes, that's our other one, we have two of them." Then Endor said" I can assure you, you will not be harmed, my father Lord DarkWar would like to talk to you as father to father, I and by brothers, and my two sisters, which undoubtedly you met, are his children." Hesitantly Michael agreed to come with Endor to talk to his father, Lord DarkWar. They both walk to the SUV and the door opens, two more brothers step out Ondor and Ionor who are just as tall as Endor looking at him then they step aside, then Lord DarkWar steps out, He looks around the neighborhood and then he looks at Michael who is froze, looking at him with disbelief because earlier, his two daughters which are over six-foot, as a matter of fact around six foot four, then his sons that are around seven foot tall, now this man who is the father who is around eight foot tall. After he get off his two sons left inside get off, a total six very tall men surrounding Michael. Michael who is now beginning to get scared looks around and then Lord DarkWar tells him" Do not be afraid, Jason's father, we are not here to harm you, I have come here to talk with you as father to father." With a little sign of relief he sighs, and then he says to Lord DarkWar "Michael is my name, and I'm very sorry for offending your daughters, to the point of provoking them." Then he continues "I was totally wrong about Jason, I assumed too much, I never gave him time to explain nothing. My god my son hates me" Then Lord DarkWar asked him "May I ask, what gave you the impression he preferred to have a relationship with the same gender as his?" looking at him he said "Again, it's under assumption, I have never seen with a girl, just hanging around with guys." Then he said to Michael "He's been with us for the past couple of days, during which, we observed him he has problems, but not like you say, no he has issues trying to please and a hard time dealing with failure, his life changed when he was attacked by our old foes, that we are now going to annihilate. We are protecting him, from this evil danger that has attacked and injured him before. He's going to help us draw them out." Michael asked "Just how is he going to help you?" Lord DarkWar said" When we asked him, if he would help, I told him, if he felt too uncomfortable with it he didn't have to, and we would not hold it against him, but we assured him he is protected either way, we needed bait to draw the evil out of the mausoleum." Michael asked "Did he agree to help?" Then Lord DarkWar said" He did, but what he said to that followed is what bothered us." Michael asked "What did he say it had to be about me, right?" Lord DarkWar said "Until we knew his problems he's been having, we thought he had a death wish, after asking him if he would help he said "You want me to seal my doom like Jim did, why not, I have nothing to lose." Michael walked to the front porch of his home and sat there quietly for a minute, they followed him to the porch and as he sat there, looking down at the grass then he looked up at Lord DarkWar with tears in his eyes and said "I drove my son too far, and for what?, he faced possible death and was injured without me knowing, and I and my arrogance did not see that. I wouldn't blame my son for not having anything to do with me, but not to the point of seeing his life as worthless and putting his life in danger." He sat on the porch looking down at the grass this time sobbing quietly so that none of his family inside the house could hear.

"We will not let any of the evil ones harm come to him, I can assure you of that Michael, my two daughters Irina and Amara will protect him." Lord DarkWar assured Michael. Nodding Michael said "Please take care of my son, I know he and I didn't see eye to eye, but I realized now how much I love him, and miss him, and misjudged him, I wish he was here with us right now." Smiling Lord DarkWar said "We will take care of him, I promise you, he cannot be with you now, and this evil that is after him will follow him anywhere, and will stop at nothing to get him, and possibly those nearby." Then Lord DarkWar said to Michael" it is time to leave, I bid you farewell, and rest to assure nothing will happen to your son Jason." With a little assurance and a piece of mind, Michael shook hands with Lord DarkWar and his sons, and they drove off back to their house to prepare for tonight. At the precinct the detective is outlining the final plans to the officers for tonight's curfew to take place. With instructions to enforce the curfew to the civilians in town, and those with knowledge of what's is truly going on, are made silence with the upmost importance, and are reminded of the possible consequences of what is to happen should any of this is to get out. As the sun starts to set and the time draws near, Jason is in his bedroom and is ever getting nervous wondering what will happen if his protectors would fail to protect him, and his fate would be that of Jims. The detective arrives at their home, and they let him in, and Jason can hear him ask them "Is Jason ready to draw them out?" and "Amara said "He is, and were ready also." Then he asked them "I've notice you have two rather large trailers you have parked inside you garage, and opening them every now and then, can I ask why?" Then Lord DarkWar said to him "Follow me, please, and Amara, can you go get Jason as well, we need him also, he is also a part of our cause and needs to be here for the recognizing." At that Jason wonders just what they have in their trailer that they need him also. Then Amara walks inside his room and says to Jason "My father has asked for your presents Jason for the recognizing." "Recognizing." Jason repeated then he followed her to the garage, where everyone else was waiting. Inside the garage are the two big black trailers, side by side. As Amara and Jason arrived Lord DarkWar said to Amara "Close the doors and any windows that may be opened so all our scent is in and not escaping out." Amara closed the door and looked for others, to close and her other sister Irina looked for any opened window to close, satisfied all is closed Lord DarkWar turns to his eldest son Ondor and tells him "Ondor, son open the first container." Ondor then opened the first trailers back door, it is an overhead door for a trailer, it's now opened and Lord DarkWar now said to everyone "Now be silence, be still, until the door is closed." Everyone is now quiet, and standing still and Jason couldn't help but get nervous again and get scared, and begins to breath faster and sweat and his heart starts to race. We is just about to panic until Irina's and Amara's hands lightly cover his chest and rubs his chest, the soothing of their hands and motion calm him down. It seemed like an hour, but not, only Lord DarkWar and Ondor knew what was inside looking at it, then they shut the door. Then everyone started to move, them Irina told Jason, you need to relax, young one, it's important that you do. Then Lord DarkWar said "Now everyone just as before is to be still, be quiet and let the recognizing take place." His time Irina and Amara was standing on both sides of Jason, in case he needs to be calm down. This time, it all went successful with no problems. Now the time finally arrives for Jason to set the plan in motion, and remove the seal, so the condemned ones can be drawn out and be ambushed then Jason asked Lord DarkWar "Suppose that bird or that dog is not in the mausoleum and instead somewhere else outside waiting, how do I outrun them?" that's when the detective said "Jason, look what we have." Jason turned to the detective and the detective showed him a case in which he opened it and showed him the contents, which is a high powered fifty caliber rifle with I capacity magazines containing special high velocity bullets with special projectiles made from the same special metal alloy their swords are made of. Then the detective said to Jason "I'll be not far off Jason, these bullets are hi velocity rounds and I was a sniper in my company and I also have my night vision specks with a silencer, these rounds have a far reach and will maim my intended target and above all it will all be quiet, they will not hear the shots fired." With a little smile Jason was at ease a little. Everyone gets in the SUV's and head towards the cemetery, during the way, there was an uneasy silence everyone knew their part, Jason is playing what if scenarios in his head of his part. They drop him off a block away from the cemetery so if he is being watched or sensed he would be alone, then they went to the other side to drop off the detective to his position and he climbed on top of an old tree with a good view, he has radio contact with the rest, everyone had a radio to communicate except Jason, who didn't know what or when they were communicating. Nervously Jason walks in through the front gates of the cemetery the gates break the silent night with a loud crick, it even startled Jason himself, as he shook off his startles' he continued walking to the back, the cemetery looks even creepier at night than during the day, but why at night he was thinking to himself. The walk seemed long and scary by the minute as he approached the back of the cemetery the mausoleum was in view, due to the poor night sky, it was hard to tell if the door was opened or closed or partially opened. As Jason got ever closer his pulse started to race and his breathing started to increase, he started to sweat in his forehead then his body, now he was not so sure if he should go forward with it. Finally he reached the mausoleum, and walked around it, to make sure no one is around it, and then he went to the front of the building, the gate was closed and he was looking right before him the bended part of the iron gate where that tall skeleton hit him with a strong force. He stayed looking for a while then he looked at the front door, it appeared to be closed, but there is only one way to find out, he had to climb in to find out. Meanwhile at the top of an old tree the detective has positioned himself with his high powered rifle and night vision specs looking at Jason with the safety off and his finger on trigger, communicating with the two SUV's, which are not too far off. Jason climes over the gate then he ever so scared goes to the front of the door and feels if the door is opened and feels again to make sure, now he knows it is closed, so he reaches for the emblem and before he does he looks around to make sure there is no dog no bird looking at him, so far so good nothing then he pulls the emblem off, but this time it's stuck, it will not budge, so he pulls out a screwdriver from his pocket and he tries again. This time he feels it working its way loose, then he hears growling and gurgling sounds and he stops, and he turns around and it's the dead woman coming from a distant dragging something with her, Jason could not quite see what she was dragging, but it looked like a person from his view, and she is coming closer to him, coming from somewhere in town, she stops and looks at the door, and sees nobody, Jason had went around the mausoleum and hid from her sight she opens the gate and walks in, drags what she has with her and stops again to look around. At the same time the detective has his finger firmly on the trigger ready for any indication of trouble, as he waits and watches he sees Jason on the other side of the mausoleum out of her view, but it seems as she might be sensing him. She decides to, drop what she has and walk around the mausoleum and so does Jason at the same time, both move, but none see each other, and both made a complete round around the mausoleum, before Jason goes to the back from her view he sees what she's been dragging, it is that odd raggedy dressed woman who use to hang around the cemetery, still struggling to breath, and shout, but whatever she did to her, she now cant. Jason looks at her she looks at him, she tries with what is left of her strength to lift her hand to have Jason help her, but Jason hears her growling coming from around then he goes quickly to the back at the same time the dead woman comes back to her victim then she stops in front of the door and has the door opened then she goes in, with her victim and the door closes. Then Jason makes is way cautiously to the front of the mausoleum and resumes removing the emblem. Looking around to make sure no one is around or no thing, he once again starts to remove the emblem. He works and works on it finally in what it seems to take forever he removes it, but he cuts his hand in the process not really concern with the blood he puts it in his pocket then he turns to the gate, and it's closed, then he climes it, he quickly but not too obviously rushes off, and heads off out off to the cemetery. While he is walking off fast, he hears that all too familiar loud scream coming from that big bird that must have been watching him from a distant. He turns around to see where the screaming is coming from, all he could see is the trees in the cemetery, he turns all different directions, it seems as if the bird is flying all over the place. Jason's worse fears is beginning to be realized, his heart is starting to pound and his breathing escalating, and now panic is starting to set in. As he continues to walk fast as hears the screams getting louder and louder and closer the detective hears them also and stars to look for the bird as well, wanting to bring to down, for what it had done to him earlier. Jason is walking fast almost in a jogging pace, looking behind his shoulder, the night sky and darkness from the tree makes it difficult to see where it's coming from. All are still in their positions as to not give themselves away, if the condemned know they are nearby they will not attack, they will not peruse their target. For some reason this time the big bird is not visible like it was when Jim had taken the emblem, maybe it could be it is night time. Still they had to be as invisible as they could to the condemned ones, if nothing happened tonight they will pick up where they left off tomorrow, meaning Amara and would have to be with Jason back at his apartment until those things follow him and begin with him as they did with Jim. As Jason walked off the park he passed by the detective who is on the tree, he had already received instructions from Lord DarkWar to let him go to his apartment, but Amara will be there before him waiting, along with her sister Irina. With a little confident Jason had done what he was asked to do, however it was nerve-racking to hear the birds screams following him without being able to see it. The detective is following discreetly as he can, using his combat skills to move on the bird incase attack is imminent all the way down to Jason's apartment where Amara and Irina is already inside his apartment waiting. As soon as Jason arrived and entered his apartment Amara signaled the detective all is well, and he left back to Lord Dark War's house, to discuss another phase of plan. During that night when Jason took the emblem from the mausoleum, he waited in anticipation, for something to happen, so far nothing happened, then they settled in for the night, Jason let Irina and Amara sleep in his bed and he slept on the couch all through the night, till morning nothing happened. Early morning the son as not yet rise Jason woke up, and was paralyzed with a horrible vision right in front of his eyes, as he lies on the couch looking out the window the big black dog is looking at him through the window, the big head and face with red glowing eyes looking at him peering through Jason's soul with his big sharp teeth looking ready to tear up or maul at Jason's body. Jason knew at any second, this big dog can break through his windows glass and take him out of his apartment like a rag doll. As Jason tried to slowly get up, his eyes locked in with the dogs eyes, and he is in a semi trance, looking at the dog, the dog is making unearthly growl at him, then all of a sudden the dog turned to its side and looked as if it saw its end, it began to back up, as Jason is watching he is joined by Amara and Irina, who also watches the dog back up looking as to whatever is making it back up, as they keep watching they realize it's their brothers Ondor and Ryoc with a very big black tiger and its back almost as tall as Jason is unlike the other tigers that have their stripes, this is all black, his are with in hits black fur, and like Lord DarkWar and his family the tiger also has markings that move and glow on its fur its eyes will glow and when its powers are not active his eyes are not pitch black and has a heavy roar. The tiger is about ten feet long without the tail, with the tail it's around maybe sixteen feet long. Its shoulder width it about four feet, its front feet had claws they are black in color and the size of tent stakes and sharp, the same with the back legs and it looks very heavy, fast and deadly. As the big dog was backing up and still growling, Ondor and Ryoc cut it loose and it charged at the dog, it leaped with a pounce, on to the dog and it sank its claws and teeth on the dog, the dog let out an unbelievable howl, it managed to get out of its grip and the big cat started to grapple with it, whatever the dog tried, the cat counteract it, during its grappling the cat pinned it to the floor and sunk its teeth into its neck, shaking it and twisting it, and the sounds of snapping and cracking, finally it stopped moving, the tiger let go, Amara Irina come out. As they come out Ondor said" Come out slow." So they did, as they did, the big tiger turned and walked up to them and smelled them and then it rubbed its big nose against their face then they turned to Jason and said "Come out slow." Then hesitantly he comes out then the big tiger walks up to him smells him then he rubs is big nose on his face, now Jason feels at ease. As he steps out of his apartment he sees the big dog lying down lifeless on the ground with a lot of holes in and around its upper body and neck. Jason sees this dog is no match for this big cat, looking at it he wants to pet it, and then he hears Ryoc say to him "Go ahead, he knows you." Jason pets him, and the cat lowers himself more to be petted, then Jason asked "Is this was in the garage at your house?" Ondor said "Yes, that's why everybody needed to be present at its opening of the compartment and quiet." The night progressed onto morning, leaving Jason and Amara, and Irina in Jason's apartment while the rest went back to rest and discuss another possible way of attack the condemned ones can implement. Not long after they left Jason looked outside his window to see the dead dog and the dog was gone as if it got up and left, he alerted Irina and Amara. All three went outside with caution to have a better look, perhaps the dog was not fully dead and dragged itself a distant, they all looked in different directions around Jim's apartment and still no sign of the dog, not even its footprints or drag marks that would suggest it could of walked away or dragged its self away, nothing. Confused and puzzled, and for Jason's safety all decided to go in until they heard from their father or brothers. Irina called her father Lord DarkWar and told him of the dogs disappearance, bothered by what his daughter had just told him, it was clear the dog did not die or they the condemned ones were nearby to retrieve its body, either way danger was nearby, but was confident Jason is protected and could be brought to safety. Jason had never noticed the weapons Irina or Amara had in their keep, Irina had a staff like weapon that doubled as a spear and a sword, for close and distant combat fighting, and Amara had a spear with a dagger inside it for special attacks and surprises, both made from that special alloy, same as their body armor. Both women in supreme physical shape have supreme strength and have superb combat skills, and unusual height and above all, very beautiful and goddess like. Meanwhile back at the home of Lord DarkWar the detective said to Lord DarkWar of the body that was being dragged in the mausoleum by the dead lady, Lord DarkWar asked him "Why did you not try to stop her?" Then the detective answered back "I wanted to real bad, but I couldn't put Jason in more danger than what he was already in." Lord DarkWar closed his eyes and nodded, and then he said in a soft yet strong undertone "We cannot let any more innocent people be taken by these condemned ones." After he said that, he looked at the detective and all of his sons. "Yes father." All his sons responded. "Detective, you look fatigue, please rest, while we discuss another phase to deal with the condemned ones." Lord DarkWar said. Nodding, the detective said "I shall return later on, today to see what you have decided." Then he left on his vehicle. On his way to get his rest he was bothered he could not intervene with the pedestrian being taken without Jason's safety in jeopardy, before he went to rest he stopped by the cemetery to back track what he saw, being a law enforcement and military, and taken an oath to serve and protect, he felt compelled to check back at the mausoleum for what he knew he saw, he has to be careful nonetheless, he too is mortal, going up against something's immortals. The day seemed gloomy, but being a man of the law, that didn't stop him from doing his duty, he approached the cemetery and as he got closer he slowed down, and stated looking ever so closely for any sign of trouble or disturbances, as he drove up to the cemetery slowly, something caught his eye, the mausoleum, and the gate is opened, he decided to go in to take a closer look. Before he got out of his car, he took out his gun clip and checked the bullets, he has a forty five semi-automatic pistol with the same kind of alloy as the he made the bigger gun, and he managed to gather up leftover alloys to make some bullets to fit his pistol. Satisfied with his personal arson he gets off his car and walks inside the cemetery making his way back to the old part where the mausoleum is at, as he approaches he looks around and sees signs of struggling, as is someone was being dragged, and was hanging on, and was over powered, he knew it was that unfortunate victim from the night before. As he looked, as he waked closer saw more clearly the door of the mausoleum, it is open more widely than before, this is alarming for him, even though if this whole thing had not had happened, with Jim breaking the seal, it still would have been cause for some kind of concern. As he approached closer to the mausoleum, he saw out of the opened doorway comes the same dog, that was suppose ably killed early morning. He stayed looking at it, and it stayed looking at him, it began to let out that unearthly growl at him, and showing all its big sharp teeth and glowing red eyes that seem to be peering through him. The detective stopped walking and stood from a distance, not too far and not too close, and the dog, looking at him as if any moment he could charge, and jump at him, and the detective also has his pistol ready unsecured from his holster, and ready to be pulled out, at moments occasion. As if the dog was not enough, the big bird all of a sudden flew from nowhere passing the detective missing him and him ducking and landing on top of the mausoleum, there it is with a wide wing span and a beak that's black, hook like, the claws very long and sharp and black and letting out its horrific screams, now at daytime although still gloomy he can see their detailed features and sizes and he can see its nothing but pure evil. As he stood still looking at both of them, the death figure comes out and stands outside the mausoleum and stands there, the detective unable to see his face because of the hood over his face, tried to see what he can, the death figure is sizable, around eight foot tall, taller than Ondor and his brothers. The dog and the bird stop making their horrible screams and growls, and stay looking at the detective. The detective cannot believe what he's seeing before him, just as Jim had told him, them the unmistakable heavy stepping sound is heard all of a sudden, and the detective knew from his investigations that could only mean one thing, the heavy walking skeleton that assaulted Jason, and took the unfortunate others, to their doom, the heavy stomping continued and right out of the entrance of the mausoleum the horrific appearance of the tall walking skeleton with a black long coat with a long black hat appeared, just like the drawings, just like the described in the witnesses accounts of seeing this big thing, just as Jim had described it to him about a year ago when he came to the station injured to report the assault on him. There he is right in sight menacing as they say he is, and as big. The big skeleton stays looking at him and him at the skeleton, and then if not that he had any more surprises the final one emerges from the mausoleum, the dead lady who he saw at night dragging a body to the mausoleum and dragging inside of it. She comes out of the back of the rest that are standing, she looks at him and starts to growl and grown at him. She's looking at him her decayed flesh which had the appearance of long been burned, and eyes so black not even the white of the eyes are visible come to a dim light. There the detective is face to face with the same ones Lord DarkWar had executed on a stake and locked in their keep. Then the detective demanded an answer when he asked them "Where is that lady you took to this place?" For a while there was no answer, there was only stares and growls coming from them, then the detective gets on his radio and called the station for back up. He waited, at that what he didn't know is Lord DarkWar had anticipated his move and had already gathered his family with Jason. He knew the detective being a man of law cannot simply go on and as if a nothing when he knows a person was harmed or otherwise taken by force, and do nothing so he lets him do what he feels what he has to do and is watching close by, letting the police be the distraction while he and his family move into position to take on the condemned ones. Then he asked them again in a harsher manner "Where in the hell did you do with that lady you took here?" Then the big skeleton went inside for a short time then he came back out, with a body, it is what the detective had suspected, the homeless lady who appeared dead, very limb, with one hand he threw her over the gate surrounding the mausoleum at him at a high rate of speed, he moved out of the way, and her lifeless body crashed against old tombstones knocking them over and breaking some of them. At that he took out his gun and took a couple of shots at the skeleton, one shooting his body and the other shooting his hat off exposing his skull. The rest looked at the detective, then they turned and looked at him then they turned towards the detective proceeded to walk out the gate of the mausoleum towards the detective, the detective backed up and right before he could call for back again, the dog leaped over the gate and ran towards him, it seemed in slow motion or take forever, for the detective, he shot at the dog, only to graze it on the side, the dog made a painful growling cry. At the same time the death figure is approaching and so is the dead looking woman, right when they are reaching close proximities to the detective Lord DarkWar and his family appears. Then they all stop, and stand looking at Lord DarkWar and his family, dressed in their battle attire, fixing to go to war with them. However the condemned ones have surprises of their own, to whom Lord DarkWar and his family along with the detective have yet to know, is Jim who was thought to have disappear or abducted and never heard from again and presumed dead was actually in a semi state of alive, but in a transformed state, his appearance is altered, he somewhat looks like the dead woman but a lot less deader, and his gained wicked properties which gives him unusual powers and strength, but is controlled by the dead woman and the others and to made to serve them. And the condemned ones know they cannot get to Jason, but perhaps Jim will, under their control. The tall walking skeleton picks up his hat places it on his head, and hastily comes out to where the others are at, and now the battle is about ensue. There is much hatred from the condemned ones, being held in the mausoleum for a long period of time, all it took is tampering from an unsuspecting individual to unleash the evil contained in the mausoleum, but they did it so discreetly, as to not to attract attention, but sooner or later there was going to be a repeat of events. The tall skeleton pulled out his weapon of choice a big mallet with a long handle made of some kind of material yet to be identified knowing them it's likely to be just as unusual as

DON'T

their powers. This mallet is capable of smashing just about everything it hits. He holds the mallet looking a Lord DarkWar and all his sons. The death looking figure pulls out his weapon of choice a long wavy sword, capable of slicing just about whatever he hits. Then the dead woman she appears to have no weapons but her finger nails grew long, sharp and black, and will shred scratch, cut, and along with her injuries her nails carry a poison. Lord DarkWar looking at them with his power sword a mighty sword forged when the world was in chaos, during the dark times, this sword has no equal. His sons, Ondor, Ionor, Kion, Ryoc, Endor and their weapons, swords, not as powerful as is fathers, but powerful swords nonetheless, the daughters Irina, and Amara had theirs with Jason, protecting him. As they are staring at each other, the detective sees the patrols coming and makes a discreet exit to the patrol cars and instructs them to set a perimeter, and goes to his car and pulls out his fifty caliber gun, and loads it and goes back and positions himself back on the old big tree as he was the other night, out of sight and to fire at the condemned ones, who are about to wage war with Lord DarkWar and his family. As for Jason, he's kept a distance from the danger with Amara there to protect him, and Irina. Irina tells Amara, "Stay here with Jason, I have to help Ondor with that trickery evil of a witch, she might pull something on him." Then she ran off and an unbelievable running speed to Ondor's back side without him realizing. As she ran off Jason could not believe his eyes, of how fast she can run and jump and leap over things. As things begin to heat up, it is like as if they picked up where they left off, the condemned ones, with a revengeful retaliation driving force with nothing to stop them from accomplishing what they set out to do. Lord DarkWar and his family the arch enemies of the condemned ones, one a long time ago thousands of millenniums ago, they were in league with one another, till the dead looking woman who was once known as Victoria, who always like using her dark manipulating powers to lure in unsuspecting victims to their dooms, and always likes to cause a ruckus, always putting Lord DarkWar and family in a mix up, and often mix up with accusations of their back arts, till finally Lord DarkWar had to do what had to be done after his daughter Irina came close to being tried for witchery. Soon after she was caught in the act by her daughter, performing her black arts, and exposed her,

Ondor and Victoria had a love affair and ended abruptly with hard feelings. First he was angry with his sister, Irina then when he seen firsthand what she's been doing and how Irina almost got tried and possibly persecuted. His anger quickly sufficed and a stronger bond merged between siblings. As they stood silently several yards between them neither side said anything, until a snap of a twig falling initiated the conflict. The first to leap and try to strike with his sword is the death figure in the hood, his swift quick moves allowing him to maneuver himself effortlessly with his wavy sword swinging at whoever he could, at the same time the dead woman takes off, running around amuck but with a plan to mortally wound Jason, as a matter of fact, she and the rest have it orchestrated so that one of them will hurt if not kill Jason directly or indirectly. She takes off with her sharp fingernail spikes, striking every one she comes close to as soon as she takes off the tall skeleton takes off with his weapon with intention to crush and kill all of Lord DarkWar and his family he comes close to his eldest son Ondor and swings his mallet and misses, Ondor returns with a swing with his sword right to his shoulder turning him halfway, but surprisingly the skeleton comes back with a hit with his mallet and knocks Ondor off his feet at the same time hitting Irina knocking her back sending her tumbling back, sending Ondor flying several yards crashing to some tombstones. Lord DarkWar enraged sees it in slow motion, and comes to the skeleton and swings his power sword striking his torso and knocking him back towards the mausoleum crashing back through the gates and through the front door flying inside with the door de hinged. At that moment the skeleton comes out walking fast and stomping louder than ever towards Lord DarkWar, with his mallet over his head lets it down, at the same time Lord DarkWar counter acts his moves round house kicks him upwards then striking him with his sword again, but on his shoulder tumbling him back into the mausoleum. This time the skeleton stays in for a while, but not too long, he comes out again steps out, walks out a few steps and then looks back, and then to everyone's surprise another tall walking skeleton just as tall as he is, and heavy, and dressed differently, he is dressed in the times of medieval, he comes out with armor on his head on his chest, and top arms, with armor gloves, and partial leg armor, with chainmail armor under, his weapon is a battle ax a big battle ax.

Elsewhere at the same time, Irina comes back running towards the dead woman who is trying to scratch and cut and gouge her other brothers, their just about to strike her, then the big dog and bird, carry out an attack on the rest. The dog went after Jason the bird went after the detective who was hiding looking for a clear shot on the condemned ones. As he looks through the scopes he sees all that is going on, and tries to affix himself to one target, but there is too many movement, and too many crossing over one another. He all of a sudden sees in his scope the big bird coming towards him at a fast speed, as if he's going to kill him once and for all, the detective then takes a shot, right on the middle of the chest, the bird goes down, but instead of going falling down, he glides down. As soon as he lands he begins to walk around then rolls around then stops rolling, and then lays there. The detective sees him there for a while, and then he turns his attention on another target. The dog is running fast towards Jason and Amara, with the intention to maul Jason to death, and whoever is on the way, as he vastly approaches the detective fires another shot, the dog keeps running, then he firs another shot, the dog keeps running this time the dog is close to Amara and Jason and is slowing down and is growing at them, Amara has her weapon drawn out, Jason, is under her looking frightened, then the dog stops and then drops. At that a sign of relief comes from both Amara who still has her weapon drawn out, and Jason who is still under her, and accidently looks up her skirt, and Amara notices and claps her feet together with Jason in between them, hard enough for Jason to get out from under there she said to Jason "Stop looking." Jason, who just got hit still a little confused, said "I'm sorry, I didn't mean to look up at you that way, and I was looking to see if you saw me." She pulled him off of the ground and stood him up with an I don't believe you look on her face. Then they went to see about Ondor who had landed nearby. They went where they saw him land and he was not there, they called out his name, and kept looking. They looked over where the battle is taking place and saw their father facing two skeletons instead of one, they were going to get close then they heard Ondor's voice say "No, stay here Amara with Jason, protect him." They turned around and saw Ondor walking with the big cat with him Ondor had taken the opportunity to get their big cat. Jason stayed looking at the cat that was looking at him Ondor again said

"Don't be afraid, he knows you Jason." Then they both ran towards the fight taking place, at the back of the cemetery near the mausoleum. As they approach the dead woman was moving fast bouncing around randomly hitting all she could then she was stopped with a hard punch to the face from Irina, she was hit so hard she flew back hard towards the mausoleum, not quite entering the door but slamming against the from side wall, she looks around and looks for her big dog and bird and doesn't see them, until she sees Irina closing in on her, she sees past her side and there she sees in the cemetery with tombstones the dog laying down lifeless, and the bird also lifeless and then she begins to whimper, at that Irina tells her "Stop your damn crying and woman up, you wicked witch." The dead woman then points out her finger and starts to utter different words over and over again. Then Irina tells her "Quit you're jabbering and get out from behind that gate, you witch, and face me." Not far from Irina and the dead woman battling it out, Lord DarkWar is engaging the two tall skeletons, one with a mallet and one with a battle ax. As they both approach Lord DarkWar they both raise their weapons to strike at him and lord DarkWar raised his sword, and right before any moves could be made, Ondor and the big cat attacked the skeleton with the big hat, Ondor flew at him with a flying drop kick, knocking him over then the big cat pouncing on him taking his mallet away leaving Lord DarkWar to battle with the armored skeleton. Lord DarkWar swung his sword to hit at the armored skeleton, at the same time the skeleton swung his ax to block his hit. This happened a few times, the skeleton had counteracted his every move then it dawned on him, this is one of his old rivals in the old world he once defeated and sent to his keep. It's a good bet this one is looking for a score to settle with Lord DarkWar. How did he get there? When? Who summoned him here? It's quite obvious why he's here. At that time the dog and the bird rose up as if they were sleeping and went after Amara and Jason. Ryoc and Endor took off running after the dog and bird making sure they didn't reach Jason or Amara. The detective who just put them down could not believe they simply got up right after he put them down, so he re loaded. The death hooded was moving quickly side to side then was hit hard and knocked off his feet and abruptly stopped by Ionor with his sword, he stood up, and both stayed looking at one another, both with their swords drawn out. Both are facing each other and a dual is setting in place, and a fight between good versus evil. All of a sudden the death hooded caught on fire, he turned around and it is Kion who has set him on fire, not really bothered by the flames, the death hooded figure takes his outer burning hooded robe off to reveal his true inner self. He looks like a big muscular body without the outer skin covering him, his muscle fibers and ligaments showing you see his not so human eyes, his sharp teeth and an unearthly groan can be heard from him, at that he started to kick with both feet and swing with his sword at both Ionor and Kion kicking and striking with fierce energy, both brothers combating it, swinging and dodging and blocking the attacks coming from him. During that time the dead woman back up into the mausoleum, looks inside then looks over the cemetery where Amara and Jason are and looks at Irina, then she goes inside, Irina yells at her "Come out, don't hide, you always hide your works in shadows, come out and face me now." What Irina didn't know is that the dead woman went inside to summon Jim, who was thought to be long dead, was kept in a coma like state, now looks dead as the woman but not as dead, can somewhat speak, as the woman comes out, she comes out with a spiked whip and starts to swing it towards Irina, Irina is watching her every move keeping clear of her spikes on her whips and she comes out, she's letting out her evil laughs and swinging her whip at the same time. That is a deterrent for Jim was once a normal man to come out to look for Jason kill him, and possibly his friend Jeff. He comes out in dark clothing, hair all dark little longer eyes pitch black as if he had no soul, somewhat looks like him, but not. He stands different, walks different, runs different, looks different his one fair skin color tone is now that of pale gray, talks but not normal, has long black nails and is very strong, and can run very fast for a long time. As Irina and the dead looking woman have it out, Jim sneaks past them, quickly and quietly looking for Jason, to kill him, because he's not as big or menacing in appearances it will be easy for him to get close to Jason, and Amara and the other does not consider mortal humans to be any threat to Jason, what they didn't know is the dead looking lady had already had sinister uses for Jim. As the fight rages on the tall walking skeleton gets up without his mallet facing Ondor and the big cat, then out of nowhere the big black vulture drops off his mallet, and goes back towards Amara and Jason, there again with his mallet facing Ondor and now with his cat. He swings his mallet at Ondor but Ondor moves too quickly, the first time the skeleton happens to get him but not this time. Ondor now is keen on keeping clear on his attacks and counteracts his moves. Meanwhile Amara and Jason is aided by Ryoc and Endor, they see the dog coming again, they look for the bird, and the bird is nowhere to be seen, then without warning the bird comes stealthy and from Amara's side and picks him up, and starts to fly off, Jason trying to break free, only gets the claws in deeper in his upper ribs and pelvic area and is in agony. Trying to yell or scream, Jason could not, due to his pain coming from the claws and his previous injury, the detective could not take a clear shot without risking serious injury to Jason, that could kill him, then out of nowhere another a bigger bird than the vulture attacks the vulture with precision, only attacking the vulture itself, punching and gouging and tearing hole after hole without harming Jason, then finally the vulture released Jason, Jason freefell a distance, caught by the bigger bird that looks like an oversize falcon dark on color. The falcon comes down gliding ever so gently, and lands with Jason softly landing on the ground, unconscious Amara quickly attends to his wounds, she sees a blood, coming from his chest, and pelvic where the vulture had grabbed him and flew off with him. The vulture with the last of its life, glides down and then crashing down tumbling onto tombstones, topping a big monument type stone on top of it, there it stayed. The big dog was already at close distance to Amara and now injured Jason, with Ryoc and Endor, in front of Amara and Jason. Amara yelling "Take it out!" At that before both brothers Ryoc and Endor could act the dog's top head exploded leaving the dog walking around confused then it finally dropping. Amara and her brothers looked up to where they thought they saw something come fast, it was the detective on top of the old tree he was the night before watching Jason, giving them the ok, he had a clear head shot of the dog. Then out of the midst of battle comes Jim walking but discreetly fast as if he was scouting for something, then he sees his target, Jason who is lying on the ground still unconscious with Amara at his side. He decides it's not the time to strike, granted he has now wicked powers that make him stronger, faster, and much more than the mortal man but these immortals are much bigger and stronger than he is, and is likely to notice him before mortal man will so he takes an alternative action, and turns a different direction and hides from view. Ryoc and Endor now seeing Amara and Jason are not in immediate threat, they move on to assist the others to fight the condemned ones. Seeing that the big bird and the big dog had been killed and probably down for good the dead lady in in rage again, and screams, in anger still with her whip trying to hit Irina with every stroke she took towards her. The dead woman threw a lash that caught Irina by her hand and caused her to throw her staff weapon on the ground and making cuts on her hand, with this the dead woman begins to make a menacing laugh and begins to pull harder causing the whip grip to tighten and make the cuts deepen and Irina starts to yell, Amara sees this and is desperate to help but cannot leave Jason. The dead woman then utters more words and then the homeless woman that the tall skeleton had threw to the detective began to get up and walk fiercely towards Irina, she picks up the staff weapon Irina had dropped and begins to walk to Irina to stab her with it, then without warning, Irina activates her powers, her markings begin to move and glow, her hair begin to glow, as so does her eyes a hum, then she does a powerful roundhouse kick to the homeless woman who had the weapon to her chest, knocking her over twenty feet high and thirty feet away causing her to stop moving. Then she turns to the wicked dead looking lady still with the whip attached to her hand, Irina grabs the whip with blades and pulls on the whip, and pulls the dead woman towards her, the dead woman cannot believe this, much to her shock, Irina is much more stronger than what she had possibly thought, and the wounds were superficial, leading her to believe she had injured Irina and her defeat in on its way. The dead woman begins out of panic pulling and tugging on the whip, in hopes to do some damage, but her attempts has proven futile. With a quick powerful pull Irina pulled the dead woman towards her, causing her to slam against her armor on her chest, both women stood there face to face, with Irina undoing the whip from her hand, the dead woman looking at her hand still active with power with her markings glowing and moving. The dead woman quickly turns and starts to run towards the mausoleum Irina picks up her staff weapon makes it to a spear and throws it at her, the force of the throw lifts her a few feet off the ground pinning her from the middle of her torso to the wall of the mausoleum. The death figure who had taken his robe off, saw and was enraged even more and let out an unbelievable unearthly howl or yell, the two waling skeletons during their fight turned and saw the dead woman now pinned against the mausoleum wall. Now there was only three left of the condemned ones, the two walking skeletons and the no skinned death figure, seeing this Amara calls the detective and asks him to watch over Jason, so she can help with the destroying of the remaining three. The detective agreed, and climbed down, and watched over Jason, who was barley started to coming around. "Don't, move Jason." The detective said. Jason stopped he still had his eyes closed and let out a light grown. When Amara left Jim who was hiding now saw the opportunity to take Jason out, now that the others are occupied, he now has a chance to do what his master wants him to do. Jim comes out of hiding looking around, and approaches Jason and the detective he quickly pounces at the detective and knocks him over, and starts to hit him, during which he growls and breaths hard, and hits the detective one last time. Leaving him dazed, then he turned to Jason and begins to him to cause his death, he kneels down, where Jason is, covers his mouth to suffocate him and prevent him from yelling, Jason with enough strength to hold off from getting suffocated, struggling, getting overpowered, as is seemed his life is hanging then all of a sudden Jim looks up and gets hit hard with a butt of a rifle, Jason looks, it is the detective, the detective continues to hit him with the butt till he gets off, then he swings his gun like a bat knocking him off, falling not far from Jason, the detective rushes to his aid. "Are you ok, Jason?" The detective asked "Thanks to you." Jason said. Then the detective looked up around to look for Jim, and he is gone nowhere to be seen, for the moment the detective is not concerned, he's armed and will shoot, the once human named Jim, the detective gets on his radio and puts on a look out for Jim. At that same time Amara rushes to join Irina, both go to join their father and brothers fighting the three remaining condemned ones. As Lord DarkWar fought the armored skeleton, and his eldest son Ondor fought the other skeleton and his other sons Ionor and Kion fought the skinless death figure, the remaining sons came to their aid Ryoc joined Ondor to fight the skeleton with the mallet, Endor joined his father, Irina and Amara made sure nothing short of a surprise would happen from the condemned ones. Lord DarkWar instructed his son to keep his distant from the fight. Endor keeps his distance, but is ready, the skeleton swing his ax to hit Lord DarkWar, Lord DarkWar moved and returned with a power punch to the jaw causing it to de hinged, the skeleton took a couple of steps back then stepped forward this didn't stop him with his jaw crooked, and he kept fighting. Then out of nowhere Lord DarkWar activated his powers, is markings began to move and glow, and so did his hair and eyes, the skeleton swung his ax only to be caught by Lord DarkWar, the skeleton tried to pull it back then thrust it, but it was to no avail. Lord DarkWar took it away from him, now it is a boxing match, the skeleton started to swing with his armor covering his fist, Lord DarkWar blocked all of his attacks and then landed his hits on the skeleton, causing it to break and crumble with every hit DarkWar gave him, finally Lord DarkWar does a power round house kick and kicks the armored skeleton in the middle of the chest plate armor causing him to go to pieces, flying back towards the mausoleum. Then both Lord DarkWar and Endor go to the others to assist in their fight. Ionor and Kion fought the skinless death figure, all three are moving fast, and Ondor and Ryoc are fighting the skeleton with the mallet. While the skeleton is swinging his mallet, and the skinless death figure is swinging his sword, Jim is on his way to his friend Jeff's house to kill him, as per desire of the ones controlling him, but the detective had already put out a look out on him with the patrols his appearance is not too hard to miss, and the likely places he's going to. The day is going by fast the detective had a gut feeling sent a patrol to Jeff's home, this is likely place hell look for, so a patrol car is sent to Jeff's home without Jeff knowing about it, and not knowing the danger he's about to be in, by this time, the day had already passed in to early evening, the fighting in the cemetery had lasted more than expected, by the detective. As sure as the detectives feelings are correct, Jim had made his way, to the neighborhood of Jeff's looking and waiting for an opportunity for Jeff to be seen, Jeff who was told the other day about a curfew, wanted to go outside one last time, before he was to settle in for the night, he was one of the few that knew the real reason why the curfew was in effect, so he stepped out and out of nowhere it seemed Jim came into view, looking at him not saying a word. At this moment the police got off their patrol and called for backup, Jim is seen at Jeff's place, and now they are at a short distant without Jeff noticing with their guns drawn out closing in. much to Jeff's surprise he sees what looks like his friend Jim but a little different, and says his name in an asking manner "Jim?" Still looking at him, Jim stays looking at Jeff with no emotion or words just looking at him. "Is that you, Jim, is that really you?" Jeff asked. Jim stepped closer then out of the brush and trees the police yelled at Jeff "Jeff, get away from him, he's not your friend, he looks like your friend, but he's not." Looking ever so confused Jeff turned to the police and asked "Who is this, then?" Cocking their guns pointing their gun towards Jim, they said "Jeff come our way now." Jeff only took two steps and with fast speed Jim grabbed him by the neck and swung him to the ground and grabbed his arm and broke it, Jeff yelled in pain, the police fired at Jim, who was on top of Jeff, Jim then picked him up put him in front of him, and they stopped firing at Jim. Jim had Jeff up by the neck behind his head, Jeff was already blacking out of the pain. The other patrol cars arrived and surrounded Jim who was still holding Jeff. The police said "Jim put him down now and back away or we will kill you." Unaffected by their remarks Jim still had him, Jeff who was in pain but still conscience asked Jim "Why are you doing this to me Jim, don't you remember me, we've been friends?" All Jim did was let out an unearthly growl and started to speak another language unheard of, then six officers waited for a window of opportunity then they rushed them, knocking Jeff off, and shooing Jim, they cuffed and tied Jim with shackles he is still alive and moving, and still talking that other language, then they check on Jeff who is barely conscience he suffered a broken arm and a fractured neck, he is taken to the hospital and Jim is taken into custody into a holding cell. Meanwhile at the cemetery the fight rages on and the sun is beginning to set to evening. Ondor and Ryoc are moving sideways with the tall skeleton walking sideways along with them, until there at the front of the mausoleum, with the mallet, he is swinging his mallet at them they are moving out of the way, at which the big cat had went to the back and climbed on top of the mausoleum preparing to pounce on him. At about the same time Ionor and Kion are battling the skinless death figure with his wavy sword swing at both of them not too far from Ondor and Ryoc battling it out with the tall skeleton. In the nearby big tree the big falcon hides, and is looking for an opportunity to strike, at the same time, looking at both at the big dog and vulture for any signs of them coming back to life and trying to attack. Both Irina and Amara watch as their brothers battle it out with the condemned ones for the last time, as it appeared in slow motion, all sons who are battling with the remaining condemned ones look at their father one by one, all got the nod of approval to activate their powers to fight. As they each one by one turned around to their facing fighting the remaining condemned ones, and activated their powers, as this began to happen, the detective who was some distance away still could see what is happening, he saw the brothers fighting with the skeleton with the mallet activate their powers, Ondor activated his powers his markings started to move and glow as so is his hair and eyes, along with a hum, Ryoc followed with his powers, his markings a different color started to glow and move as so did his hair and eyes along with a hum. The other brothers, battling the skinless death figure Ionor a different color other than his other brothers activated his powers his markings start to move and glow as so does his hair and eyes and a hum and Kion, also a different color activates his powers like his brothers his markings start to move and glow as so does his hair and eyes and a hum. Ondor faced the tall skeleton, the skeleton swung his mallet, Ondor caught his mallet, the skeleton pulled back and Ondor did not let go or did not move, then the skeleton, pushed towards him, and again, Ondor did not move then he snapped the handle to the mallet close to the mallet head, causing the skeleton to step back, then looking at the broken mallet the skeleton then swings the handle at both brothers, and this time Ryoc catches the handle and again the skeleton pulls and pushes with Ryoc not moving. Then with a power pull, he pulls the handle takes from the skeleton and jabs him straight into his bone face causing it to fracture from the nose eyes place, then as soon as Ryoc hit him Ondor jabbed him on his jaw causing it to fly off. As soon as his jaw flew off, he started to punch fast at Ondor and Ryoc, and kicking, Ryoc caught his foot, then Ondor gave him a power close line, causing him to slam hard against the ground, in which, the skeleton got back up and this time both brothers power roundhouse kicked the skeleton causing him to fly over the mausoleum and slamming into the pinned to the wall dead woman crushing her and going to pieces. The final condemned figure the skinless figure is fighting and still swinging at that time evening is upon them and still some light from the sun, Kion approaches with his powers activated, instead of putting his weapon down and catching the sword, he transfers some of his powers to his sword, his sword stars to illuminate almost the same color as his color is, with the already hum his powers are making his weapon starts to make a metal upon metal sound his brother Ionor does the same thing, his powers illuminates his weapon and it also makes a metal against metal noise then Kion swings it at the skinless death figure casing his weapon to shatter to pieces, after the shattering of the sword Ionor swings his sword striking the skinless death figure at his center torso, causing him to drop, but not for long, he got up, with his deep cut visible and started to fight again. He picked up what is left of his sword and before he could strike again Kion thrust his sword in to his chest and kicked his sword out of his hand, then Ionor swings his sword and decapitates him. His body stays standing for a while swinging his arms trying to strike still, finally it falls motionless. The big cat jumped off the mausoleum and the big bird flew in from his place of view, joining the family for destroying the remains of the condemned ones. All of their bodies are gathered to a ditch that is dug, and the remains are burned to ashes in the ditch with a special fire that will keep burning for days to make certain their bodies are ash. It is now night the fight is over, the condemned ones are destroyed, the family now had fulfilled their obligation to protect people from this evil, the detective is still with Jason and tells Jason he'll be back, Jason is still, in and out of consciousness. The detective approach Lord DarkWar and shook hands with him, and acknowledged not he or the police could have defeated the condemned ones. During Lord Dark War's conversation with the detective, Amara went to attend Jason's wounds, and said to her family shell be taking him to their home and cleaning his wounds, so no infection will spread. She picked him off the ground gently and carried him to their vehicle and Irina drove them home. The dispatcher called the detective and informed him of Jim and Jeff, Lord DarkWar and his sons went with him to the hospital, to see about Jeff's condition. As they went inside the hospital some police were are in the lobby along with, Jeff's immediate family, father, mother, two brothers, and

---

three sisters was waiting, for what the doctor had to say. Jeff's families received a call from the police about Jeff in an incident and are in the hospital and are worried about him. The detective walked in and greeted the family and goes to see about Jeff. The detective checked with the doctor, who had also checked Jim, and Jason, told the detective "He will be ok, he will not be able to use his arm for a while, and his neck, and he'll have to wear a brace for a while also, we like to keep him overnight for observation." At that the detective nodded went to see Jeff, Jeff opened his eyes and asked him" Where's Jim?" The detective said to him "Don't worry about him now, your safe, he's in the police station." Then he asked "Can he have visitors?" the doctor said "Sure, but don't excite him too much." Then the detective went to the lobby to inform Jeff's family they can visit him. During the time of their waiting to hear about Jeff's condition, his family did not notice Lord DarkWar or his family, respectfully, Lord DarkWar and his sons let Jeff's family see him first. Then they walked in to Jeff's family surprise they too are overtaken from their appearance and size. They see Jeff is not surprised to see them, and greets them, then introduces them to his family. Then Jeff has a look of a question on his face, Lord DarkWar knows his question and nods at him saying "Yes, and they are no more." Smiling Jeff closes his eyes. Meanwhile at Lord Dark War's home, Irina and Amara are washing up, Jason is in bed sleeping with his wounds cleaned and dressed in pajamas, he finally wakes up and looks around, and sees he's back at their home, and his wounds are cleaned and dressed, and he's been bathed, and in pajamas, and now he starts to get embarrass just thinking during his unconsciousness who picked him up and carried him, who took his clothes off, who bathed him, who dressed his wounds, who saw him naked, who dressed him, and put him to bed like a little child. Jason got out of bed and walked to the gathering room where Irina and Amara is at, and sat down, "Careful you do not tear your stitches, Jason." Irina said. Then Jason looking down asked "How did I get here?" Then he slowly looked up and Irina and Amara looked at each other smiled and Amara said "You were carried here." Jason put his head down and slowly shook his head. Then he looked up at them, they were looking at him and were going to ask who did what to him, but decided not to. Then he put his head down and said "Nevermind I'm embarrass as it is to ask." Then Irina and Amara get up and sit down beside him on both sides then they kiss him on his cheeks and Amara says to him "Jason everybody needs help from time to time." Then Irina lifts Jason's chin and tells Jason "If you really must know, we both took care of you, it did not feel right to leave you with untreated wounds, and those are deep wounds." Then she kissed his forehead, and then Jason smiled and said "I'm going back to bed and thank you for everything." Then he got up and started to walk as he did he turned around and Irina and Amara smiled at him. Then he went to his room and went to bed, he didn't quite go to sleep, he just couldn't help but wonder about them and how his life would have been if he hadn't met them. Then he wondered where they lived, this house is a rental for their stay, but where is their real home. At the same time at the police station, a man formerly known as Jim is in a holding cell chained down. The detective informed them he'll be in the morning, and ordered the officers to keep him in custody until he arrives. In the time the detective will arrive at the station, the officers called in a psychiatrist to communicate with the man formerly known as Jim. It was early morning hours of the night, the psychiatrist arrives the officers and staff told him of the situation, and his growls and spoke another language and told him he is chained up because he's incredibly strong, they show him a photo of him how he use to look like before he disappeared, and just resurfaced a few hours ago, acknowledging their input he nods and goes inside the holding room with two officers and begins to talk to Jim. As he talking to Jim, he sees bullet holes in his shirt, and looks for the wounds, and sees none, it would appear as if he healed. He is looking down all the time the psychiatrist is talking to him. Then the psychiatrist called him by his name then he slowly looked up, instead of looking into what he thought was going to be human eyes, he looked into something else. He slowly looked up at the psychiatrist and then he looked into his eyes, and looks into almost deep pitch black color, the whiting of his eyes, are of a medium gray, his eyes once had their natural color but is almost black, and is almost animal. This made the psychiatrist nervous, his hair longer his skin from a flesh tone beige to a pastel gray, his fingernails black, his teeth are dark gray and somewhat sharp. "Jim, can you hear me, can you understand me?" the psychiatrist asked him. Then Jim looked into his eyes and a sense of cold filled the room and he began to growl at him, then he stopped then he looked and slanted his head then he started to speak a language he's never heard before. A little nervous the psychiatrist asked Jim "Can you speak English, can you communicate?" Then Jim spoke again in that language, then he started to pull the chains holding his arms down. He started to growl louder, and it was freakish, then he snapped one of the chains, and that's when the two officers escorted the psychiatrist out of the room. Eight officers entered the room to sedate him, and then secure him again. Morning arrived and the detective is on his way to the station to see about Jim, who is in the holding room, but first he is on his way to the hospital to check on Jeff, he should be ready to come out, he wanted to ask him questions concerning his attack from now his former friend Jim. As he entered his family is waiting and he asks them with their kind permission he'd like to take Jeff to the station to get a statement on his attack and questions, with a family member to accompany him to take him back. They agreed, Jeff's brother Hank accompanied him to the station, he followed him in his car, and then he was with him in the station. After a few questions and a statement given by Jeff, he was almost free until one officer informed the detective they are having trouble with Jim asking him questions and all he's doing is talking in another language, and they have no idea what he's saying. The detective got up and Jeff asked to go with him, he still wanted to go see his friend Jim, so the detective let him and Jeff's brother followed. As they headed back Jeff was looking at his friend Jim through a mirror glass in a room, Jim is locked up to a chair, in shackles and cuffs. He turned to look to the glass, and was looking at Jeff, and started to speak in the foreign language. The officer that was in the room with the detective and Jeff and his brother said to the detective he has no idea what he's saying. Looking at him a cold chill ran though Jeff's spine, he said to the detective "I think I know who might understand what he's saying." The detective asked him "Do you know someone who can speak this language?" then Jeff said "I know a linguist, who I met at a seminar a while back who spoke to Jim before he disappeared, about the emblems inscriptions, and he read them to him, he might be able to understand him." The detective looked at Jeff and said "I didn't know Jim had spoken to him about this." Nodding to the detective Jeff said "He did, he wanted to know the meaning of the inscription on the emblems and the gentleman deciphered it for him." Then the detective asked him "Just who is this linguist you're talking about?" then Jeff said "His mane is Brandon Stewarts, he's from Europe, I have his number." At that the detective gestured him to give him the number Jeff pulled his car out of his wallet and gave it to the detective and the detective went to his office to make a call. While the detective was away making the call Jeff and his brother and an officer was still in the observation room looking at Jim, and the thing he has turned into. Jim was looking at his friend his eyes began to tear up and is remembering the times he had together with him, he was one of his best friends, all the good times and not so good times, but still they were there for each other, now this thing that looks like him almost killed him. The police shot him and it didn't seem to faze him any, he also felt cold not only physically cold but none humanly cold as if he had no soul. As Jim was in the holding room he saw a vision of the dead woman but in her beautiful appearance before she got condemned and burned to stake, he came to him and spoke to him in the language he was speaking, he was responding back, with Jeff and his brother and the officer watching from the observation room. Jim looked as if he is speaking to someone and is enchanted by it, and Jim sees the woman and her beauty and she caresses his face and chin and then goes. Jim then sits still and a sense of anger sets in him and starts to pull on the chains holding him down. The detective comes back and tells the officer and Jeff "Well I'm luck, Mr. Stewarts is in town, and is at the local collage and will be here shortly." Then the officer informs the detective on what has happened when he was away. The detective notices Jeff and the look on his face and tears in his eyes, and tells Jeff to sit down with him so that he could tell him something about Jim. As they sat down the detective said to Jeff" Jeff as much as you would like to see and speak to your friend Jim, this is not Jim, he's something else, he's not your friend who use to be Jim, he's something else, until we can understand what he's saying well have an idea." Jeff looked down at the floor and tear drops fell to the floor he is comforted by his brother who is beside him. Then Jim stands and looks at the window to the holding room and the looks at Jeff, then detective said "I know Jim you want to speak to him, probably reminiscence some times, but it's not a good idea, it's too dangerous for you." Nodding Jim agrees and looks at him for the last time, he is about to leave until Mr. Stewarts walks in and greets the detective and Jeff, and asks what he can help him with. Then the detective points at the observation window to the holding room and asks him" Mr. Stewarts, do you know what he's saying?" Mr. Stewarts looks through the window and much to his shock he sees it's Jim, and he asks the detective "Is this Jim, the one who disappeared about a year ago?" Nodding the detective said "Yes he is, and he's not who he used to be," then the detective asked Mr. Stewarts "What did you translate for him, I know it has to do with the mausoleum but what exactly is it?" then Mr. Stewarts said "Let me go to my car, and get my book and I'll explain everything to you detective." Mr. Stewarts goes to his car and gets his book he had shown Jim before his disappearance, and then he comes back. He opens the book and dhows him the emblems and their inscriptions, and their meaning, then the detective asked him "Did you ever tell Jim to put those emblems back?" looking at the detective with utter grief Mr. Stewarts said "We discovered it was too late, even though he put back the emblem, the ones inside were still going after him." Then he showed the detective the inscriptions and read them to him "He who breaks the seal is doomed." Then the detective looks at him and then he points at Jim and says "Well, it makes perfect sense, look at him, he's messed up or should I say doomed." Then Mr. Stewarts looks at Jim once more and shakes his head and said "He must be tormented or in utter control, of the ones who took him." "Yes he is." The detective said who was also looking at Jim. Then both the detective and Mr. Stewarts go in to try to communicate with Jim. As they go in Jim looking down at the table top then Mr. Stewarts says to Jim "Good morning Jim, how are you?" Jim who is looking at table does not responds and still looks at the table, then Mr. Stewarts asks him "Do you know where you're at?" Then Jim looks up at him with those inhuman eyes and lets out an unearthly growl then he begins to speak to him in that foreign language and at that Mr. Stewarts knows what he's saying. Mr. Stewarts starts talking back to him in the same language and try to carry on a conversation. After about ten minutes talking to him, the detective and Mr. Stewarts go back out. And the detective asks "What did he say?" Then Mr. Stewarts said "He's saying you cannot contain him for long, his master will come for him, and will destroy all who has captured him and contained him." Then the detective said "Well I've got sad news for him, his master has been destroyed by the keepers of the mausoleum." At that Mr. Stewarts turned to the detective and asked him "How do you know his masters been destroyed, this book I have indicates that these are immortals and has been around for a long time, nothing can destroy them, they are just contained, by the ones who put them in that mausoleum?" At that the detective said, "It's a long story, and believe it or not, the ones who did put them in there, did come back and destroyed them, all of them." Mr. Stewarts looked at the detective and had to ask "This stuff is pure legend, it's so old even doubts had set in to as if they really existed or not, but I have tangible proof that the mausoleum has kept some kind of evil inside until our unfortunate victim broke the seal." Then the detective asked "How would you like to meet the ones who put them in there and destroyed them?" Then Mr. Stewarts in utter excitement said "Why certainly, I would love to meet these." Then the detective said let me first arraign our friend to a court hearing and have him move to an institution where he could be looked after, and try to be helped." Then Mr. Stewarts said "Oh yes of course, he needs a lot of therapy." So Mr. Stewarts waited for the detective and finally arraigned Jim to a mental institution then the detective let Jeff's brother take Jeff home. As they left the station a van was there to pick up Jim, as they lifted him up on a gurney sedated with drugs he turned to Mr. Stewarts and the detective and said more things in that foreign language, Mr. Stewarts stayed looking at him. Until they loaded him up and took him away. As the van drove off Mr. Stewarts stayed looking as if he was bothered and the detective asked him "Are you coming?" And Mr. Stewarts said "Um yes, of course." As they drove the detective noticed an eerie silence from Mr. Stewarts, and he asked him "Are you ok?" Then he said "I'm fine." They finally arrived at lord Dark War's house, they got off then they knocked, and much to Mr. Stewarts surprise he saw for the first time, what he has been reading from his book, and the keepers of the condemned ones. As they walked in he was introduced by the detective to the sons, then the daughters, and finally Lord DarkWar himself. They got acquainted with each other, then he proceeded to ask questions, the family was happy to answer his questions then finally he said to the detective, in a concern tone "What Jim told me before he, got taken away is there are others seeking to avenge him and his masters." Then Lord DarkWar said to Mr. Stewarts "Have no fear, we have battled countless and countless of foes, who sought us to defeat us and all who tried and fell to my sword and family." Then Mr. Stewarts showed them his book he had possessed for a long time, it's been in his family for generations. Then he checked to see what their response would be. Then Lord DarkWar said "These book are written by people who were there first hand to witness our justice dispensed on the ones who are mightier and took advantage of the weaker species of humans, humans had no defense over them and turned to us to defend them. You have one of many books written of our kind who defended mankind over untold evil. That is one of many chapters written about us and our kind, you must have had an ancestor who was there and witnessed the event." After a lengthy conversation with the DarkWar family Mr. Stewarts bid his farewell, and left with the detective back to the station. Then there the detective thanked Mr. Stewarts for his help and Mr. Stewarts welcomed him and he went back to the collage where he is staying at to finish giving his lectures of world languages. It is now noon time, and the detective is now rapping up his final details to his cases he worked on and now going to lunch. At Lord Dark War's house Jason finally wakes up and finds Amara and Irina looking after him, and asked him if he is hungry, Jason said yes, so they take him to a local diner to eat a meal, there he sees an old rival, his sisters lover, and a very rude one at that, she also partook in the rumors of Jason was gay, Jason and her did not liked each other. And she decided to give him a hard time for the other day and her not being able to come no more to his sister's house. What she didn't notice is Amara and Irina was with him, he just happens to come in first to the rest room, now she has her opportunity to retaliate against him. As he stepped out of the rest room he heard a voice telling him "Hey fag, what you are doing here, no fags allowed." He turns and it's her sister's former lover and she's pissed, before Jason could answer she threw a hard kick towards Jason's genital area, hitting him hard, Jason in pain can't even yell, fell to the ground, and now she said "Yeah that's right faggot, you don't even like girls you homo." Jason said "You stupid bitch, I'm not gay, you are." Then she said to him while he was on the ground "Yeah I came in with a guy, everyone saw me, so they will believe me over you, you, came by yourself." She was about to do something else to him, until she heard a voice "I wouldn't do that If I were you." At that she turns around and sees two tall women over six foot, looking at her, all the other people stopped all turned to look at Irina and Amara, who looked very angry. "Who are you?" She asked them, looking at them she's moving back from Irina then Irina quickly grabbed her arm and twisted it and made her apologize to Jason, she was no match for Irina, "Now apologize to him now, you sorry excuse for a woman, who knows this kind gentleman will not hit a woman." She resisted at first till Irina started to put more pressure, she started yelling "You're hurting me." During that time Jason was on the floor curled up, until Amara comfort him, she saw he was bleeding from the stiches near his pelvic area at that Amara was fueled with anger, and her markings started to glow and move and so is her hair and eyes with a light hum. At this the girl was terrified, and was paralyzed with fear, her guy friend she came in with went to see what the commotion was all about, to his surprise, he saw two very tall beautiful goddess like women, one had his buddy friend by her arm and the other had Jason picking him up. Amara was about to dismantle her on Jason's behalf but Jason said "Don't she's a sexually confused and angry young woman." The girl was frozen out of fear looking at Amara and her illuminated appearance, all Amara did was give her a good shove, which made her fly across the room crashing to other spectators. All the guys in the café were awe stricken with their goddess like beauty and strength, and one of them said "I don't think that guy is gay, look at the babe, dolls he's with." They decided to leave, on their way out they out Amara who is still angry grabbed the girl she showed and made her look at the bleeding she caused, and told her "You think this is lady like, doing this, how would you like if me or someone else did something like this to you?" Irina then told her "Were going to have him tell the authorities, you are no woman, you are despicable." Then they walked out, then Jason fainted, they helped him in the SUV and then they drove off. At that everyone looked at the girl who kicked Jason, and now they know about her, and wanted to know more about Jason and his new beautiful friends. As they drove back to their house Amara again picked up Jason like a child carefully as not to hurt him and rip his stitches that haven't been already been ripped. After a good part of the day went by, Jason finally came to and again woke up cleaned and re stitched, this time Amara and Irina had his meal in their house for him. He checked himself and shook his head again he knows the girls already saw him without clothes. Jason asked Amara, "When are you going to go back to where you come from?" "Why do you ask?" Amara asked him. "I'm going to miss you very much." Jason said. Amara smiled and said "We'll leave with in the week, back to Europe." Then Jason said I wish you could stay more, I wish you were my girlfriend." At that Amara sat down next to him and held his hand and kindly told him" Jason look, it's not possible for you and I to have a relationship, we can be friends, but that's it." Jason asked "Why, I'm male you are female." Then Amara said "Jason, were two different species of humans, you are mortal I'm immortal, the intimacy would kill you, you wouldn't survive the process, as my kind of species we need three days to rest after intimacy, Jason your body couldn't take it, and I care too much for you to harm you." "Oh." Jason said with utter surprise. Jason began to think, the power they have the strength, the size, the majestic, and that glowing power they have when they're going to hit a target, perhaps she's right, it will be too much for him. Then Jason asked Amara "Can I come with you, to where you live, only to visit?" Then Amara looked at Jason, and asked him "Why would you want to come with us to visit, your home is here." Then Jason said "I need time away from things around here, you've seen how things are here for me, I need time to think things without being bothered by everyday heckling." Then Amara thought, nobody has ever wanted to go with them back to their home, let alone be with them. Then she asked him "Just how long do you intend to stay?" Then Jason said "As long as it takes, for me to learn how to deal with these ever growing problems." Amara said to Jason "I'll be back." Amara left and was gone for about a half an hour and then came back, and then she said "Jason you can come, but remember, we can't have any relationships except friendship, agreed?" Nodding Jason said "I really need good influence and perhaps lessons on how to defend myself." Amara smiled at him, after a couple of days of taking care of loose ends finally the time came for their departure to Europe. As they were waiting for their flight to arrive, Jason's father arrives and looks a little distraught and walks to Jason and asks him in a quiet tone if he could have a word with him before he goes. Amara watches Jason talking with his father, Jason showing little emotion and his father who is about to break down emotionally, finally his father nods and leaves with a handkerchief blowing his nose and wiping his tears walks off and turns one last time to look at his son, then he leaves. Jason then walks back and sits quietly and waits with Amara and Irina, Amara asks him "Is everything ok Jason, with you and your father?" Nodding Jason said "Yes, I turned down his welcome back home, I'll never feel welcome, after he treated me and all the things he said to me, now he wants to make things ok." Amara said "He looked sincere when he was talking with you." Then Jason turned to Amara and looked at her with a doubtful look and said "Amara, one small act of half way decent gesture does not make up for a life time of neglect, what you and Irina got to see is the tip of the iceberg of what that man is capable of doing." Nodding Amara smiled and then the announcement of their flight came, they now got ready to board the jet plane to Europe. As they boarded the plane Jason looked back at the town he grew up in, since there was mostly negativity he not going to quite miss it, but looked forward to going to Europe to spent time with his new founded friends, they headed towards their destination and finally landed in Europe where other vehicles were waiting for them, Jason was a little confused it was like getting limo service to where they live, but to Jason's surprise, all this belonged to Lord DarkWar and his family, not only is Lord DarkWar a warlord he's also a tycoon, and a very powerful person who lives with his family in a beautiful majestic castle fortress, that is private and is well guarded, and has servants. Jason is awe stricken, and now Amara and the rest welcomes him to their home. As they entered their home they were greeted by their mother, who did not go with Lord DarkWar, she had to contend with local affairs with their servants, as she approached every family member hugged and kissed their mother, and Lord DarkWar gave a passionate kiss to his wife the queen, then they introduced her to Jason, she greeted him with friendship, she is just as beautiful as her daughters, only she has golden blond hair and eyes, and also markings like the rest of the family she's a little taller than her daughters, and like her daughters she has a goddess like appearance. This is where Jason spends a few years learning how to do martial arts to learn how to defend himself taught by Amara's brothers and her father they know about the incident in the restaurant involving a girl who kicked him, and of course schooling, Amara thought his high school education was inadequate so she enrolled him in a private collage that would come to their home to educate Jason. Within a couple of years' time Jason transformed from a vulnerable person to a savvy person with wits and his body also transformed from a no tone body to an Olympian like fine muscular toned body he even found love with one of the girls who is hired help that worked for Lord DarkWar, now their serious about their relationship. Amara is happy for Jason he's found happiness, Amara and Jason had developed a close relationship like brother sister relationship along with the rest of the family. From time to time Ondor, Ionor, Kion, Ryoc, Endor would test out Jason's martial arts skills along with Irina and Amara watching along with Lord DarkWar and his wife and Jason's girlfriend his future wife. Jason's life has transformed for the better, now he has class he can defend himself and others, has top education, now love. The time will come when Jason will come back to his home where he grew up and take up residence there again, along with his future wife, but will still have strong ties with Lord DarkWar and his family. In a matter of speaking Lord DarkWar and his family is family to Jason.